THE FRAUDULENT BROAD

THE FRAUDULENT BROAD

JAMES L. RUBEL

CUTTING EDGE

ISBN-13: 978-1-957868-96-7

Published by
Cutting Edge Books
PO Box 8212
Calabasas, CA 91372
www.cuttingedgebooks.com

CHAPTER ONE

AT first he was just another big lug with not too much future. There were thirty-two working out of that branch. They showed up each morning promptly at eight. They listened in various stages of boredom to the manager's pep talks, sang songs that extolled the virtues of the Keen Kleaner, picked up their sample cases and left to ring doorbells, get insulted by hired help and bitten by unfriendly dogs.

Edna Goes was sort of an order taker with a desk close to the manager's office. The salesmen handed their sales orders to her, she okayed the commissions due, made out a voucher and the cashier cashed it. If you were bringing in the orders regularly, you were treated royally. If you didn't. Edna Goes looked down on you as though you were a pariah.

If she knew Danny Slick was a member of the organization, she failed to show it. He'd liked her looks from the first day, the dark and glossy hair, the equally dark eyes, and the figure under the severe white blouse and the dark skirt. He'd mumbled good mornings and received nothing in return but a cursory look. At least not until he began to lay orders on her desk with frequent regularity.

He'd been there close to six weeks when she surprised him one morning with the greeting, 'Hello, Dan! Lovely morning, isn't it? A wonderful day to be outside working instead of slaving over a desk in a stuffy office. Lots of luck today.'

It was so unexpected all he could manage was a mumble as he joined his team in the salesroom. Sam Colter, who was his team captain, noticed his dazed look, and he punched him playfully in the bicep.

'I recognize the symptoms,' he chuckled. 'Don't let it go to your head. Edna treats us all the same way. It's her way of giving you a pat on the back for your efforts.'

All that day as Dan pounded the pavements and made his demonstrations Edna Goes was never out of his mind. That greeting, small as it was, had reacted on him like a shot of benzedrine. He craved to lay more orders on her desk and see and receive her smile of appreciation.

By four he was back, standing in front of her, watching her hands as she checked his sales, noting the incredible blackness of her hair, and the pair of large imitation pearl earrings, the only jewellery she wore with the exception of a signet ring.

She finished checking the orders and made out the vouchers. She handed them to him as she said with a ghost of a smile, 'You're really on the ball, Dan. That makes five orders so far this week. No one else has even come close. Congratulations. At the rate you're going, you'll be a millionaire before you're forty.'

The way she looked at him, the way she cocked her head on one side, the lift to her lips, filled him with quick and unexplainable awkwardness. All he could manage was a stupid grin, a grin that he knew was that way.

'Just the breaks, Miss Goes,' he mumbled. Sudden strength came into his voice and he stiffened to ask the question he'd been wanting to ask. 'It's more than I can spend. I don't suppose—' His voice trailed off and vanished as a lump came into his throat. He had wanted to ask her for a date. Now he cursed himself silently for his timidity. Something in her eyes made him feel as embarrassed as a teenager with his first date.

'My friends call me Eddie,' she told him quickly. 'I'll be all finished in half an hour. Perhaps you'd like to buy a lonesome little girl a cocktail?'

She was not only pretty, he decided instantly, but a mind reader. The Golden Slipper was around the corner. It was a hangout for the Keen Kleaner salesmen when the day's work was done. He not only wanted to buy her a drink, he wanted to show her off to his competitors. It proved that he was the fair-haired boy. The thought of having her close made him forget his timidity.

'Why not make it cocktails and dinner too,' he suggested. 'After spending the day cleaning filthy rooms for lazy house-wives, I could use a shower and a change. How about meeting me at the Golden Slipper around six? We can go on from there. Or I can pick you up?'

Her eyes brightened: 'That would be nice. Should I dress?'

He wasn't too sure what she meant by that and he said, 'Use your own judgment. Only remember I don't own a monkey suit.'

Her laugh was bubbling, infectious. 'Then I'll just wear a suit, Dan. The Golden Slipper at six.'

He collected his commissions from the cashier, took the elevator down to street level. Still walking on a pink cloud he came close to having his trousers shaved off by a passing motorist who yelled at him, 'Go back to Iowa, you jaywalking knothead.' At any other time he'd have retorted in kind.

The face that looked back at him as he ran a comb through his sand-coloured hair after his shave and shower would never take any beauty prizes. The more he looked at himself and considered it, the more he realised what a lot of brass he'd had to ask Eddie Goes for a date. She was class. He was still just a big farm boy, not from Iowa as the man had guessed, but from the great state of Texas.

Still she had accepted his invitation. Perhaps she was the type who liked big bruisers with rugged mugs. He had heard of women like that, met a few of them in fact during his service days.

Eddie was almost as prompt as he was. He had no more than ordered a Martini very dry when she came in. All Dan could think of was a luscious blackberry pie. She looked that tasty. The dress was black satin and she had a white woollen stole over her shoulders. Her glossy hair was combed back into a swirl of a chignon.

Until the drinks came she played on the table's top like it was a set of piano keys, chatting of business and telling Dan what the other salesmen were doing. She could remember every order that went across her desk, even the names and the addresses.

'You keep hitting the ball, Dan,' she told him, 'I happen to know that Corcoran is slated for the district managership, and it's the custom for one of the present crew to step into his shoes. Until you came along Norton was top man. He's the one you'll have to beat.'

Tom Norton was in a team ahead of Dan in point of service. He was a natural salesman and a good closer. Corcoran was always holding him up in front as a fine and shining example. Dan had never liked Norton's looks. He thought Norton was a poser, a large phony.

The waiter brought the Martinis and they clinked glasses. 'I couldn't imagine anything sweeter than being your boss, Eddie,' Dan acknowledged. 'Only I don't believe I'd leave you sitting in the outer office.'

'And where would you put me?' she purred.

His grin was as broad as his mouth was big. 'Where I could look at you, where else?'

She shook her head and shrugged. 'I'm not that photogenic and I'm a terrible secretary. My shorthand is atrocious. Nor can I type fast enough. That's why I'm where I am.'

They had another pair of Martinis and moved to a night spot where they had a calypso band and Mexican food. Eddie was just the right size and she could dance. She didn't do the rhumba from two feet away. She did it Cuban style, close, the way Dan had learned it down in Panama when he was in the Navy.

When the music stopped they stood there, momentarily absorbed in each other, their bodies still touching.

'You're good,' she whispered, her voice faintly tremulous. 'Where on earth did you learn to rhumba like that?'

'From a Senora down Panama way,' he stammered. 'She was about your size and colouring.' Then he added quickly, 'Only not as pretty.'

A small frown tugged at her forehead. 'What on earth were you doing down in Panama?'

'Navy,' he shrugged. 'A Frogman.'

Suddenly he noticed that they were alone and that the orchestra was taking a break. Reluctantly he took her back to the table. He thought she deserved a little more information on his past life and he told her.

'The Senora worked in a cafe down in Panama City. It was one of our regular hangouts. Her husband owned the joint. No one made any passes at Senora La Sala. Alonza was not only jealous but quick-tempered and fast with a shiv. We all played it safe.'

She cupped her chin in her hands and stared at him. He knew that something was going round and round in that head of hers, but he couldn't figure what. It made him faintly embarrassed.

'Did anyone ever tell you before that you're a handsome devil?' she asked suddenly through faintly narrowed lids.

Dan Slick was startled. He managed a timid smile. 'Let's be honest, Eddie. No man with a face like mine could ever be called handsome. I've got a mirror at home. It doesn't lie.'

She took the cigarette he lit for her, inhaled and let the smoke exhale in a drifting curl through her lips while her eyes focused on the burning tip.

'I don't mean handsome in a pretty sense,' she explained. 'I suppose a lot of people would call you an ugly man. Yet you have the type of face that a lot of women like. There's a quiet ruggedness and a streak of charity. I'll bet you have a lot of sympathy for the underdog. I'd also be willing to bet that if you walked down the street with five other men, that a panhandler would single you out for his first pitch.'

Her ability to read those facets of his character seemed to him almost uncanny. He had always been a sucker for the poor sap trying to make a living the hard way. He grinned at her and shook his head.

'Anyone who took that bet would be crazy,' he told her. 'I can walk down the street with a dozen guys and the panhandler always singles me out. Dogs follow me like I was the Pied Piper. But not cats. They know I hate them and they keep their distance.'

'Why single out cats?'

'It goes back to my tender years. The old man gave me a duckling for Easter. We had a ring-tailed cat who was a good mouser. She killed the duckling. I haven't liked cats since.'

They had the special dinner with enchiladas, salad and coffee. The enchiladas turned cold while they danced. Dan just wanted to hold her in his arms. She was willing. Romance, smoke and Martinis changed the look in her eyes. They took on a smoky cast. They decided suddenly that they needed some fresh air.

Dan's car was no high-powered, late model. The cracked leather seats had plastic covers. Eddie was kind enough to mutter as he helped her in, 'This is nice, Dan. I like convertibles better than coupes.'

The ocean was forty minutes away. Dan didn't have to show up at the office. He had an appointment ont in the sticks to demonstrate a cleaner. But Eddie had to punch the time clock. By the time they had reached the Pacific, she was sound asleep with her head pillowed against his shoulder. The midnight newscast came on after he had parked in front of a public beach.

Eddie stirred a little, her eyelids fluttered open, and she stared blankly up into Dan's face. Her voice when she spoke was as soft as a caress.

'Where am I?'

'What a memory!' he chided. 'You're in Danny Slick's Rolls on Highway 101 south of the Palisades. Would you like a smoke?'

Her hand moved up and her finger tips followed the shelving ridge of his jaw. 'It must be terribly late. You need a shave.'

'Five o'clock shadow,' he told her. 'And it's not so late. About ten after midnight.'

'What on earth are we doing here?' she demanded peevishly.

'Breathing fresh air and thinking.'

'Of what?'

Her fingers moved up the back of his neck and combed through her hair. 'Short, isn't it?'

'A butch,' he said. He put his arm around her shoulders, pulling her in closer when she raised no objection. 'I've been thinking mostly about you. I've never been in love before. I'm not sure I am now. But if it isn't, then it must be a fever. It wouldn't take long for me to reach the point where I couldn't get along without you. You grow on a guy, Eddie.'

'It's the night air, Dan.' She giggled and looked up at him. 'Maybe you ought to kiss me. I've been wondering all evening what it would be like.'

'Then cease wondering.'

He tipped her chin up with his fingers. Her lips were cool to the touch and tasted of raspberry. She pulled her head back and stared at him, her expression one of bewilderment.

'You kiss like a first-timer, Dan. Either you're playing hard to get or you're trying to confuse me. Let's go home. I have to be at the office not later than eight thirty.'

If the kiss had been disappointing to her, the feeling had been mutual. Hers had been on the indifferent side, as if she might be testing. It had been hard to judge. He turned the ignition key and started the motor.

In a surprised voice she asked, 'What no objections?'

He looked at her and grinned, 'None, Eddie. You want to go home, that's where you go. You want to try some other joint, that's okay too. But we'd hardly get inside before they'd kick us out.'

'Where do you live, Dan?'

It could have been a suggestion. He gave her the benefit of the doubt. He said, 'A rooming house over on Seventh. Two flights up. It's no place to take guests. If I brought a female into the place the landlady would burn my ears off?'

'I'll buy you a nightcap.' She pulled her compact out and began to rouge her lips. 'I live alone. Self-service elevator. Top floor. A kitchenette. Living room, bedroom and bath. No roommate. Maid service and ice water. 2238 South Hobart. South of Pico. When you get to Vermont, turn right.'

She closed the compact and leaned back, watching him as he left the parking area and tooled on to the highway. When they reached Santa Monica Boulevard and straightened for the long drive east, she put her hand on his arm.

'You're a real right guy, Dan. I like you. I might even fall in love with you though I swore I'd never be that crazy again.'

'Burned?' he asked with a sidelong glance.

She nodded, her fingers curling and uncurling on his sleeve. 'He was no damned good. Ran away with a bottle blonde and left me holding the bills. I went to Vegas and got a divorce. I figured all men were like that. Until I met you.'

'And now you're not so sure?' he laughed.

'Frankly, no.'

Her fingers left his sleeve. Nothing more was said. The more Dan thought about her the more he felt sure she would fit into the pattern, his pattern. He had always had a yen for brunettes, dark ones like Eddie and Senora La Sala. Eddie was pretty, but not dumb. Nor was she too smart. Apparently she had come up the hard way as he had. That made them kindred souls. She'd been burned once. So had he. If he continued to sell cleaners as he had been the last four weeks, if he could latch on to that manager's job, he'd be in clover. With that he could carry his end. Apparently she had the apartment. But would she go for a set-up like that without a wedding ring?

CHAPTER TWO

PROMPTLY at eight Dan walked into the office to pick up a new cleaner for his demonstration. He could have used a drink. The combination of gin, wine and Mexican food had left him with a mouth full of feathers. He had a pint in his locker which he kept for medicinal purposes. He didn't have time to even taste it. Corcoran spotted him, called him up to the platform to hold him up as an example of what a man could do if he used his legs and brains.

'Slick made two sales yesterday,' he announced. 'Excellent trade-ins and cash on the line. Didn't even have to call me for advice. One of these days when he has the time I intend to have him demonstrate our DIG MORE DIRT sales talk'

Dan saw Norton down in the front row with a sneer on his face. He knew that every word of praise Corcoran gave Dan hurt Norton's ego. Up until that morning Norton had been the favourite. He resented anyone else rising to that special spot.

'Slick's been hitting the ball hard,' Corcoran continued earnestly. 'He doesn't take No for an answer. He's made five sales this week and this is only Thursday. A man can't do that grousing around. It takes shoe-leather and grit. Read over your booklets. Learn that demonstration by the heart. Punch those doorbells. Use the Master Door Opener. It works. Maybe not every time, but a good percentage. And if you manage to make a sale, try and pick up a prospect or two. It's like a chain reaction. Women tell their friends when they have a cleaner they like. Even if they don't buy, they may like your looks enough to give you a friend's name.'

He stopped momentarily for a breather while his glance moved around the room, pinning each salesman to his seat. It was good psychology. It made each salesman think that Corcoran was talking directly to him.

'I'm going to take this opportunity to tell you something that's strictly off-the-cuff. Two months from today I move out of this office and into a District Manager's chair. One of you will have the opportunity to take over my job. Seniority will have nothing to do with it. It makes no difference how long a man has been with the firm. In order to handle my job a man has to know every angle of the selling end. He has to know how to close. Therefore the one I recommend will have to be the top salesman.'

He was a tall, lean human dynamo with dark hair and a pair of cold grey eyes. He was all business. The boys who kept the machines moving out of the warehouse, who had the cash rolling in were his buddies. The ones who didn't, got called on the carpet and had their rear ends painted with verbal turpentine until they did or quit. Corcoran had no use for the ones who just managed to squeeze by with occasional sales.

Tom Norton had been top man and still was. But Dan was creeping up on his record. He didn't like it. Norton had joined the company nearly a year ahead of Dan. He had sold a competitor's cleaner before. He knew the ropes. Now he had the added incentive of the manager's job dangling in front of his nose. He would work even harder to stay at the top of the heap.

Norton wasn't the type to pull any punches either, Dan knew. He would do everything he could think of to discredit his opponents. He'd try to horn in on the other salesmen's territories. That part didn't worry Dan. Two could play the same game.

For every prospect Norton sold in Dan's stamping ground, Dan swore he'd sell two in Norton's.

The meeting was over at eight-thirty, after they had sung the Keen Kleaner's anthem. Eddie was at her desk, rouging her lips and nodding pleasantly to her favourites as they went by her on the way out. Much to Dan's surprise and bewilderment he had been demoted back to the peasant class. She made it clear that she wished to forget the previous evening. Her manner was patronizing. The temperature had dropped from torrid to freezing.

She condescended enough to give him a nod and a frosty smile. That was all.

Dan did a slow burn. A hangover, he thought, was excuse enough for ill-temper. But this reaction had none of those symptoms. She was friendly enough with the other salesmen. He decided that if and when he made the grade and took over Corcoran's desk, the situation would be reversed. When that time came he'd make her do a little squirming.

For three weeks the relationship remained the same. Either at the end of the day or first thing in the morning, Dan turned in his orders. Eddie checked them silently, made out the vouchers and gave him no more than civil answers.

He didn't have to ask her how the other men were doing. The company made that glaringly clear to one and all. There was a jungle scene set up on the stage. Each man had a niche. If you ended the week with no sales they hung a cut-out of a skunk up for you. If you made only one sale you had a monkey. But if you had an elephant, a tiger, a giraffe, or a polar bear, it proved you were really selling. If the king of beasts hung in your niche you were top man on the totem pole.

Norton was slipping. For two weeks running Dan had the lion. The other salesmen were beginning to take sides. Norton had his quota of adherents who hoped that he would win the managership. Dan had his. The rest had given up all hope of winning the contest.

Dan's most enthusiastic fan was an older man who had been a door-to-door salesman most of his life. He hated Tom Norton.

'Beat that phony,' he urged Dan. 'If you don't the chances are good he'll have you pounding the pavement looking for another job. He'll grease the road for you.'

Norton's adherents claimed that Dan was lucky or was chiseling sales in other bailiwicks. They had to have some excuse to appease their egos. Norton spent a lot of time hanging around Eddie's desk. Dan hadn't reached the jealous stage, but he didn't like it. It smelled of skullduggery to him. Dan was sure of it when Corcoran called him on to the carpet.

'You're doing a terrific job, Slick,' he said. 'But I don't like the tales I hear about you. You know the rules. Norton claims you're muscling into territory that is his and some of the other men. They claim that's the real reason you make so many sales. Let's hear your side of it, I haven't heard any beefing from you.'

'If you'll take the trouble to check my sales,' Dan told him, 'you'll find that every one is legit. I make it a point to get prospects from those I sell to. They can be anywhere in the city limits. You know that. I seldom have to ring a doorbell. My customers make the appointments for me.' He handed Corcoran his book with the names of prospects and the addresses. 'Take a copy of those names if you like. Check them off as I make sales to them.'

Corcoran glanced at the book and nodded. He handed it back. 'Okay. I'm satisfied. But in the future try to get something in writing to prove your side.'

Dan was sure that Norton was behind the sly insinuations. He decided to ignore it, figuring he could afford to. But Norton had other ideas. He didn't like the licking he was taking. The more Dan side-stepped, the worse it got. Norton even managed to convince Eddie that Dan was a heel.

It had to be settled and it came to a head after a very tough and disheartening day for Dan. He'd had three seemingly hot prospects, each at long distances from the other, each one outside his regular territory. Everything had gone wrong. In one woman's living room the carpet had been so moth eaten that Dan had pulled the nap completely off the carpet's backing, leaving an ugly bare spot that nothing could hide. The woman had threatened to sue the company.

The second prospect had been nearly as bad. He had sweated three solid hours cleaning an entire bungalow only to have the woman tell him to come back after she had talked with her husband. Dan knew that answer by heart. He had guessed wrong. She was just another chiseling female who was too lazy to clean herself. Why should she when there were salesmen around anxious and willing to do the job?

The third prospect was something else. She was in her early thirties, bronze hair tied into a pony tail, long jade and gold earrings looping down from fawn-like ears, topaz eyes with sweeping black lashes and blue eye shadow to enhance their depth. She was an armful in an off-the-shoulder chiffon blouse and a flaring large-flowered peasant skirt in ballet slippers.

She held a highball in her hand. She looked Dan over with faintly smiling lips and opened the door wide when he told her who he was. She smelled pleasantly of some exotic scent that suited her looks.

Dan laid out his tools and went to work. He cleaned the oriental rug in the living room, dumped his bag and felt like swearing. Nothing came out but a hair or two. He wondered if the machine bad lost its suction.

She giggled and waggled a finger at him. 'That wasn't fair, Mr. Slick. That rug came back from the cleaners this morning. I wanted to find out if they did a good job. Can I fix you a drink? It's cocktail hour someplace and I hate to drink alone.'

It was against the rules to drink with customers but he was too tired and disgusted to refuse. After the previous two prospects he needed a lift.

'I could use one,' he told her with a weary smile. 'For a minute there you had me worried. I was afraid my machine was a lemon.'

While she was out in the kitchen making the drinks, he cleaned the davenport and as per custom dumped the bag's contents into three separate piles back on the cushions. She raised her eyebrows in horror when she saw them.

'I don't believe it!' she exclaimed. 'All that crud couldn't possibly have come from that davenport.'

He assured her that it had and got out his order book for a fast close. She ignored it and handed him a highball instead.

'Sit down and relax,' she suggested brightly. 'Of course if you're in a hurry or have another appointment—' She left the sentence unfinished, but the disappointed look she gave him told him that she was a lonely woman and she craved companionship.

He was getting the run-around again and knew it, yet he didn't care. As long as her husband didn't come home and find a cleaner salesman guzzling booze in his house, there was no danger of his being reported. Mrs. McGowan didn't look like the kind who would report a man for an infraction of the rules.

He tucked the order book back in his coat pocket and took a sip of the highball, still standing and looking at her. She was, he decided, after a few moments of quick appraisal, something extra special in females. Her cheekbones were high and faintly shelving, her mouth was full and rather long, her nose too retruse to be considered beautiful. Yet the arrangement of features had been done by a master's hand. She was not a pretty woman in the strict sense of the word. Yet she was outstanding and tauntingly seductive. She affected him in much the same way Eddie Goes did.

He suggested that he didn't wish to impose on her hospitality and she insisted that he sit down close to her. She told him that her husband was out of town and that he too was a salesman of sorts.

He switched the cleaner on long enough to clean the dirt off the davenport and when he turned back, he found her sitting on it and patting a spot next to her. Highball in hand he sat down, sipped at it, and for a while they engaged in small talk. Mr. McGowan wasn't really a salesman although he had started that way. He owned his own company, but he was away a good deal, checking on the branches.

'We moved to Brentwood only a few months ago and I haven't many friends as yet. It's been rather lonely with Clifton away so much.' She handed him a faint sad smile. 'I do hope you don't mind, Mr. Slick. I'm not keeping you from some other appointment, am I?'

He assured her that she wasn't. He told her that he wished more housewives would meet him at the door looking as lovely as she did. 'You'd be surprised at how some of them dress, Mrs. McGowan. They're enough to scare a man to death. They meet me in everything from pyjamas and bathrobes to toreador pants. I don't mind the pants. On a slim woman they look good, but when the rear is on the beefy side, then they look like the hind end of a yellow cab.'

She giggled, 'I know what you mean. Let me sweeten your drink. You can't possibly fly on one wing.'

He fired up a smoke and when she returned, he lit one for her. She curled up at one end of the davenport, legs tucked under her full skirt. He sat at the other end facing her.

She told him that her husband didn't approve of her associating with men her own age, that he was old, almost seventy, a nice guy but strict and Victorian in his ideas.

'I can't go to cocktail bars alone. I get tired and bored with shopping. When I married Clifton the differences in our ages didn't seem so great. Now that he's ten years older he tires quickly. I'm only thirty-one. He used to be a heavy drinker. Now I call him one drink Clifton. More than one and his kidneys go on the rampage. I might add that life is rather dull around these diggings.' She smiled through partially closed lids at him. 'Are you married?'

'No woman's wanted me bad enough,' he assured her.

'You're too modest,' she giggled. 'With your looks you could go a long ways.'

He chuckled. 'Now you're pulling my leg. My face isn't my fortune.'

She excused herself and left the room. She came back a few minutes later and stood with her back to Dan, looking at the mirror. He looked up and caught her reflection. She was watching him with speculative eyes, lips slightly parted, her bosom rising and falling as if with some inner ferment or anticipation.

The two highballs had dispelled his weariness and her conversation had given him a lift. He glanced at his wrist watch, noted the time and told her, 'My office closes at five. Perhaps I had better return tomorrow.'

She turned to face him, her eyes pondering some thought that had germinated behind the thick copper hair.

'I'm sorry, but I won't be home tomorrow. It's my hair dresser day. Shampoo, wave, massage, the works. Couldn't you report to them by phone? I have nothing but time on my hands now. No engagements, nothing. Surely you don't want to miss a sale. As my husband always says, you have to strike while the iron is hot.'

She moved across the room and stopped to look down at him. She was close enough for him to touch. He could smell that exotic scent. From the way she stood he knew that if he reached out and took her in his arms, she wouldn't object. It was plain to read in her eyes.

'When you first arrived,' she said, 'you mentioned something about a corpse in the mattress. It sounds utterly, fantastically ghastly, but if there is such a thing, you must show me.'

He'd never had a prospect offer her affection so openly and he was angrily embarrassed, not at her, but at his own lack of intestinal fortitude. He had to fight to keep his hands off her. He knew she knew it. She was trying to break down his defences without becoming too brazen or bold and offensive.

His thoughts were revolving and he couldn't think of any ready excuse that would sound plausible. Yet some presentiment of danger ahead if he succumbed to her entreaties held him back.

'Maybe if I had another drink,' he suggested hopefully. 'I really don't have to call in. I can make my report in the morning'

Her entire face brightened as if someone had suddenly opened a hole in the ceiling and focused a Kleig on her head.

'Wonderful!' she breathed ecstatically.

The moment she was out of the room, Dan jumped for his machine and case. He scooped the whole business up in his arms and fled for the door. He yanked it open, leaped out, slammed it behind him and legged it for his car. He didn't look back. If he had he'd have seen an hysterically laughing red-head who screamed profanities after him from the open door while a Great Dane almost as big as a Shetland pony stood beside her and slobbered.

CHAPTER THREE

DAN didn't breathe easy until he was a full block from the McGowan residence. It was too late to either go to the office or call. He fired up a smoke and headed downtown for the Golden Slipper. In the back of his mind was the hope that he might see Eddie and get his nerves unwrapped. The McGowan woman had class and plenty of it, but she wasn't for the likes of Daniel Slick.

Reaching the cocktail bar he sat on a stool and ordered a Scotch over the rocks. The clock on the back bar said six. While he waited for the drink he kept remembering the red-head, the way her eyes had shone, the bronzy colour of her hair and the way she had filled out that peasant costume.

He wondered if she was a real hot number. He wondered too how early she started drinking. Was she a before-breakfast tippler or did she have the strength of character to wait until her husband had left? Would it be safe to return for another demonstration? He doubted it. She was undoubtedly furious that he had run out on her.

He tried to picture her husband and failed miserably. All he knew was what she had told him. Clifton McGowan was in his early seventies. He was the head of a big sales organization that had a lot of branch offices. Perhaps an outfit like Keen Kleaners. They didn't manufacture their own machines. They contracted to have that done.

The bartender brought his Scotch. Dan lifted the glass to drink. He caught Eddie's reflection in the back bar mirror. She was sitting in a booth with Norton. On a sudden impulse Dan called the cocktail waitress over and told her to serve the couple a drink, compliments of Dan Slick. He knew it would get Norton's goat. Norton didn't like the idea of being obligated to Dan even to that extent.

The result was all that he had hoped for and more. Norton's face screwed up into a tight mask. He gripped his lower lip between his teeth and glared at Dan's back. Eddie said something to him. He frowned and shook his head vehemently. She frowned right back and apparently told him where to get off. Norton shrugged and called the waitress. She crossed to where Dan sat and told him that the lady and gentleman would like to have him join them for a drink.

Dan paid his check and moved over to the booth. 'Greetings, fellow slaves,' he said.

Norton frowned, said nothing. Eddie was more friendly than usual. You're late. You failed to report in. Did you have a good day?'

'Terrible,' Dan told her with a weary grin. 'The first prospect is going to sue. I pulled off the nap from her moth-eaten carpet. The second was a chiseling housewife who wanted a cleaning job done for free. The third—.' He shook his head and looked lugubrious—'The less said the better. Your territory, Norton.'

'What was her name?' Norton growled.

'McGowan,' Dan answered. 'Built. Thirty-one. A strawberry parfait in a peasant skirt and topped with a cherry. The red hair didn't come out of a bottle. Topaz eyes.'

'How'd you get by the dog?' Norton gave Dan a scowl.

Dan was surprised. 'Didn't know there was one. I didn't see or hear him.'

'And you didn't sell her?' Norton looked very relieved and hopeful.

'Nor do I intend to try again,' Dan told him. 'She's not my cup of tea.' He chuckled and added, 'I doubt if your technique will work either.'

'Why, you—' Norton started to climb out of his seat. Dan shoved him back with the flat of his hand.

'Not in here, friend,' Dan warned. 'But there is a parking lot outside. If you're game?'

The weight of Dan's hand made Norton livid. He called Dan a profane name, flung Dan's arm aside, and jumped to his feet. He was faster with his fists than Dan had expected. His fist caught Dan along the side of the head, sent him sprawling backward out of the booth.

After that Dan heard a woman's scream and a man's bellow of unadulterated fury. Something exploded against his skull. The world turned inside out, then grey and dark. When he finally opened his eyes he thought he'd been over Niagara Falls. Some one had done a very thorough job of wetting him down. Even his shoes squished with water. Then he saw the waitress backing away, her pale eyes wary and frightened.

The next one he saw was Eddie. She was off to one side and behind the waitress. Norton stood beside her. His hands hung at his sides. An empty beer bottle hung from the fingers of his right hand. Dan could smell the beer on his clothes.

The floor was covered with a crimson-dotted asphalt tile. Dan had walked across the floor and never before noticed its colour or texture. He saw a lot of things from that prone position he had never seen before. The front of the bar was stained underneath from spilled drinks. It needed a cleaning and some fresh coats of varnish. It was scuffed clear to the wood where the customers shoes had scraped it.

Dan put his hands down and raised himself on his palms. The silence was so thick he could hear his shoes squeak as he moved. His head was one huge area of pain. He got to his knees and his brain started to function more normally. The bartender was watching him carefully, warily. He was an old-timer at the Golden Slipper, but one that Dan had never troubled to get well acquainted with. Dan was a comparatively new client. Norton had been around much longer. It made Dan wonder which of them the bartender would side with if the going got rough again.

He climbed slowly to his feet, holding to the back of the booth for support. His eyes focused on Eddie and Norton. Eddie's reaction he wasn't sure of. Nothing definite showed on her face with the possible exception of faint pity. Norton was playing the waiting game, uncertain and cautious.

Dan decided that the slugging was okay. Norton had packed a swift and deadly punch. Dan hadn't expected it. But cracking a man over the head afterwards with a partially filled beer bottle wasn't according to the rules as he knew them.

But if he followed through as he wanted to do, what were his chances of leaving the Golden Slipper on his feet. The bartender might call the police. Most of them did when a brawl started. In that case Dan felt sure that he'd be the one to end up behind bars. The prospect wasn't pleasant, yet he wondered how he could keep his self respect if he didn't retaliate, if he let Norton walk out without a mark on him.

He made up his mind. Corcoran wouldn't like the news that his two best salesmen had been bar-fighting. It might kill Dan's chances of ever getting that manager's job. He took his handkerchief from his breast pocket, wiped a smear of blood from his lips, and forced a vacuous grin to his face. With a nonchalance that he was far from feeling he stalked out, ignoring Eddie and Norton like they were no more than pieces of furniture.

He reached the sidewalk. He heard high heels following him. He heard his name called. He paid no attention. He kept right on going into the parking lot and to his car. Eddie caught up with him, grabbed at his sleeve.

'Why are you sore at me?' she panted. 'I didn't hit you. That was a dirty trick, Dan. I tried to stop him, but he hit you too fast.'

He turned around to face her, remembering their first night together and the way she had felt in his arms. Then memory flooded back and he recalled the way she had treated him the next morning and every day since, like just another one of the hired help.

'I'm not sore at you,' he answered stiffly. 'Let's just say that I'm disappointed. I figured you had better taste. I thought you knew a first class jerk when you saw one. On the other hand, maybe you're the kind who likes to bet on a sure thing. Maybe you feel you're backing the big winner. You could be right, but somehow I don't think so. Not yet. Not until the sales are all in and the decision is made.'

She didn't say anything. She looked at him with wide eyes and tears silvering her lower lashes. If he hadn't been made from his demonstration and the way the women had used him that day, he might have melted. He was still crazy about her but stupidly and stubbornly determined not to let her know it. He plucked her hand off his sleeve and let it drop.

'In any event, Miss Goes,' he said with grave politeness, 'let's keep our relationship on a strictly business plane. What you do or how you act is your affair. You can have drinks with the garbage man if you choose. On the other hand, what I do is my business. But you might carry a message to Mr. Corcoran. If you will be so kind? Tell him that Danny Slick has a very early appointment with a red-head. Good night.'

'But you said—?' She looked surprised and irritated.

Dan chuckled. 'I changed my mind. After what Norton said about the dog, I decided I'd go back and give it the old college try again. Mrs. McGowan is about the most luscious dish these old eyes have feasted on in many a moon. Even if the dog chews the seat out of my pants, even if I don't make a sale, it will be worth it. Just looking at Mrs. McGowan is enough to give a man a lift and to make him dream of Paradise.'

He opened the door of the convertible, slid behind the wheel, stuck the key in the ignition and started the motor. He left her standing there, chewing on her lips, her eyes as brightly black as polished onyx.

When he reached his room, he had a shower, and put some cold compresses on his head. He decided that all the claims the vacuum cleaner people put out about house cleaning being simple were a lot of cat-fat. A woman could dig into places with a cleaner that she couldn't reach with a broom. So what? Your home was cleaner, there was no argument on that score. But you had to work twice as hard getting it that way. Dan was sure that it was a lot easier to lift up the corner of the rug and sweep the duster under it.

He was too tired to eat, too sore to dress again. He went to bed, climbed out early, and except for a slight pain at the back of his head where a lump had formed, he felt fine.

Mrs. McGowan had told him it was her day at the hair dresser's so he decided to hit the house early. It was exactly eight-thirty when he pushed the bell. No one answered, but he could hear someone moving around inside. He stepped off the porch, stared at the rest of the house. He wondered where the dog was. He tried the bell a second time and when no one answered he returned to his car and headed for the nearest drugstore.

He looked up the number, dialed and got the busy signal. Mrs. McGowan was home. He returned and parked in front of the house, watching it, trying to decide what to do. The front door opened and a man came out. He was all of six foot two, stooped a little and didn't look the seventy odd years she had claimed her husband was. Yet Dan was sure that he was looking at Clifton McGowan.

He had a better look at him a moment later when McGowan backed a new Cad out of the garage, turned and streaked by Dan in the direction of downtown. His eyes had looked pale blue and there had been a pair of pouches under them as big as Lynhaven oyster shells. Clifton McGowan was big but old. Dan felt sure that a man couldn't live ten years with the red-head without looking old. She was enough to take the starch out of a much younger man.

When the Cad was out of sight, Dan slid from under the wheel, and with his case in his hand, headed back for the front door. A great Dane as big as a lobo wolf came loping around the corner of the house, growling deep in his throat. Dan stood perfectly still, too paralysed to do anything else.

The dog came close, sniffed at Dan's clothes, at the back of his hands, at his boots and the sample case. He stopped growling. His long tail started a faint wagging. Dan touched the dog's throat, gingerly at first, then when the animal didn't object, with more vigour, rubbing and scratching it. The dog sat on his big haunches and started scratching the same spot with his right hind paw.

'The top of the morning to you, old friend,' Dan greeted. 'Is your mistress at home and would you mind too much if I punched the doorbell?'

Dan didn't have to punch it. The door opened and Mrs. McGowan stood there. She looked at Dan as if he were something that had just come out of the woodwork. The bronzy hair was in a peruke, caught with a gold pin. She wore a green house dress that was snugged in at the waist with a wide gold sash. Her feet were encased in green velvet slippers with high clear plastic heels.

'Well?'

She teetered on the high heels while she balanced herself with one hand on the frame of the door.

Dan could have chinned himself on her breath. It wasn't bourbon, Scotch or plain gin. He guessed it was Vodka. It had that strong taint of pure alcohol. It came at him in waves each time she exhaled.

'I was here yesterday,' Dan explained carefully. 'I came back to finish the demonstration of the Keen Kleaner.'

'Yesterday?'

She looked blank and her eyes focused on something behind him.

Dan explained very carefully who he was. He apparently tunnelled through the alcoholic haze for she opened the door wider and invited him in. The dog took that as a personal invitation and followed Dan. Mrs. McGowan closed the door, motioned Dan into the living room, sat down on the davenport and looked at him expectantly.

Dan opened his case, brought out the vacuum, hooked it up to the nearest outlet and began the demonstration from the beginning. He cleaned the entire oriental that he knew had come back from the cleaners, then went to work on the furniture.

The dog sat on his haunches by his mistress, watching Dan and cocking his head occasionally as some strange noise from the machine puzzled him. Dan called him over, used the brush along his back and the Great Dane did everything but roll over. If he could have purred he would have. He was in total ecstasy when the brush was moving over his chest and belly.

Mrs. McGowan lifted one eyebrow and looked owlish. 'Bren seems to love that. How much is it?'

Dan told her the full price of the machine with the tools, with the moth bag and with the spray outfit. He showed her each one. He got out his order book, wrote up the sale and handed it to her to sign. He had never felt so good in his life. Once he had Mrs. McGowan's name on the dotted line Norton would holler his head off.

She signed quickly and he tore out the carbon. There was a breakfront on the other side of the room with the lower part a desk. She opened this, wrote out a check for the full amount and handed it to him.

Dan packed the tools on to the machine and placed the excess ones in the box they came in. He thanked Mrs. McGowan heartily and told her that any time she needed service not to hesitate to call. He would come out personally.

He picked up his empty sample case and headed for the door. He heard a strange sound in back of him that startled and frightened him. When he turned and looked back, Mrs. McGowan was the colour of the bone-white drapes and gasping for air.

Dan dropped the sample case and rushed for her. He was scared she was having a heart attack. He had never seen any woman behave as she was. Bren came padding in from the kitchen whining.

Mrs. McGowan took one look at him, pointed at him and moaned, 'The dog … Bren … Get him out of here.' She gasped again and managed to whisper, 'I'm allergic to him.'

The topaz eyes rolled up into her head like a pair of window shades. Her knees bent. She folded into a heap with a rustle of silk.

CHAPTER FOUR

I T was an asthmatic attack brought on by the Great Dane's close proximity. At least Dan hoped it was nothing more serious than that. He grabbed the dog by his collar, led him to the door, pushed him out and closed the door hurriedly before the big animal could barge back in. He heard him whining and scratching as he returned to his customer.

He picked her off the floor, carried her to the davenport and stretched her out with her feet on a pair of pillows and her head down. That was the correct way to treat a faint. He wasn't sure just how to treat an asthmatic attack.

He followed the route she had taken the day before, found a powder room with some smelling salts, and an empty kitchen with coffee still warm on the stove. He turned the burner up to medium, carried the salts back to his customer and gave her a whiff of it. She opened her eyes and stared at him without recognition. He got some wash cloths from the powder room, soaked them in ice cold water, returned and placed these on Mrs. McGowan's forehead.

'Relax,' he told her. 'You fainted. You'll be okay in a minute.'

She managed a faint smile.

He returned to the kitchen, found a pair of cups and saucers and a tray. He put the coffee maker and the china on it, carried it back to the living room. He poured a cup for her, handed it to her. When she tried to sit up and reach for it, he helped her and stuffed the pillows behind her back.

For that pleasant chore he received another weak smile and a 'Thank you' that was barely audible.

She drank the coffee as if she enjoyed it. He asked her if there was any special medicine she had handy for her allergy. She told him there was a bottle of yellow pills in her bath and that they could be identified by the small red S on them.

'They're in the medicine cabinet.'

Dan got the pills for her along with a glass of water from the cooler, told her that if she felt okay, he would like to leave.

'Please don't leave me.' Her voice was no more than a whisper of pleading. But it was the smile that did something to him. Even as dopey as she was, it had a terrific kick behind it. He decided that she could be not only human, but one swell dish when the booze wasn't running her brain.

'I'll stay as long as you ned me,' he assured her. 'Cigarette?'

She nodded and he gave her one from the box, then fired it with the table lighter, then lit one for himself. She studied him through partially closed lids while she inhaled and slowly exhaled.

'I love dogs,' she told him with a faint sigh. 'But if Bren remains close to me for long, I get one of my attacks. It's only short-haired dogs like Great Danes that seem to bother me. The doctor said it was something to do with the hair. They gave me all the tests. I'm so glad you were here when I had the attack. Both the maid and the butler are off on a short vacation. For a moment I thought I was going to die. That's the way it affects you. I feel as if my lungs are closing up. As long as I take my pills regularly it doesn't bother me. But sometimes I either forget or just tire of stuffing pills into my mouth.'

She took another deep inhale and exhaled slowly, letting the smoke curl around her face. 'I think you told me your name was Daniel Slick? Do you mind if I just call you Dan? My name is

Cleo. That's short for Cleoney, not Cleopatra. It's a family name. Irish, I guess.' She smiled and added, 'That's where the red hair comes from.'

'Call me anything you like,' he told her.

She stared at him as if she was speculating on his reactions. 'I could use a little brandy, Dan. You'll find a decanter on the sideboard in the dining room. Would you mind awfully? I still feel sort of rocky. Did I hit my head when I fell?' She put her hand up to her hair and smoothed back the crown as if she was feeling for a lump.

'I don't think so. You just seemed to crumple. I figured it was an asthmatic attack. Had a friend that used to get them occasionally. I'll get the brandy.'

He didn't think brandy was the remedy, but neither was it his place to tell her what she should or should not do. He found the decanter and a set of small snifters, brought the bottle and one glass back with him and placed them on the table. He poured about two ounces for her and helped himself to more coffee when she shook her head in the negative.

'Wouldn't you like some brandy?' she asked. 'It's excellent Amontillado. Supposed to be fifty years old.'

He shook his head and told her, 'Afraid the boss wouldn't appreciate brandy on my breath this early in the morning.'

'Do you have to leave so soon?' That pleading note was back in her voice again.

Dan climbed to his feet. He knew if he stayed much longer he'd be in trouble. That same premonition came back to disturb him, nothing tangible, just the supposition that this woman could lead him into a sack full of misfortune. He had seen the husband earlier. Clifton McGowan didn't look young enough to be any match in a rough and tumble, but he undoubtedly was in the chips and could pull a lot of wires. Dan wanted that branch manager's job so bad he could taste it. He was tired of being just a door-to-door salesman. He knew he had ability and he craved for the opportunity to prove it. And beyond all else was the desire to beat Norton and to show Eddie that she was backing the wrong horse.

'I'm truly sorry, Mrs. McGowan,' he started.

She interrupted with, 'Why so formal, Dan? I told you my name was Cleo. Don't you like me? Am I so hard to take? And I bought your machine too,' she added with a sigh.

'You're a mighty easy person to like, Cleo,' he conceded and meant it. 'You're easy on the eyes and easy to take. But I'm just a door-to-door salesman. I'm out of your class. It's been fun sitting here talking to you and I'm glad I was around to be of service. I'm glad too that you bought my machine. I think if you'll run the cleaning tool over Bren occasionally, you'll have less trouble with those asthmatic attacks. And I might add that any time you need service, you'll get it promptly if I have to come out myself.'

'Maybe I'll need it sooner than you think,' she told him archly with a faintly cynical smile.

'Do you want me to tuck the cleaner away in the broom closet or wherever you keep such tools?' he asked. She shook her head and he held out his hand. 'It's been nice knowing you and thanks again for the order.'

Her hand was hot to the touch and he wasted no more time. The look in her eyes convinced him that if he stayed much longer, she would find some other excuse to detain him.

Bren was waiting on the porch and came padding up to him, hopeful of getting back into the house. Dan held him back with his leg while he closed the door behind him. Afterwards he patted the dog's head, said good-bye and headed for his convertible.

As the motor revved into life, another car slid by him, and turned into the McGowan driveway. It was a low-slung foreign job. Dan had a brief look at a thinfaced man. That was all.

Eddie was at her desk when he came in. He handed her the sales slip, picked up his voucher and went into Corcoran's office to report on the woman who had threatened to sue. When Dan finished his report, Corcoran scowled at him, scribbled something on a piece of paper, and passed it across the desk.

'Give this to the cashier,' he said icily. 'Turn in your sample case. You're finished, Slick. As of now.'

Dan stared at the manager, his eyes hardening, his anger climbing like a thermometer with a match under it. Norton, he was certain, had talked. Even Eddie had probably put in her two cents. And Corcoran hadn't even taken the trouble to hear both sides of the tale. He was condemning Dan without a trial. Dan started to open his mouth and tell Corcoran what he thought of such treatment. Corcoran beat him to the punch.

'I heard what happened last evening in the Golden Slipper, Slick. I won't have my salesmen mixed up in saloon brawls. It gives the company a bad name. I've come to the conclusion you're a trouble-maker.'

Dan's guts were suddenly a ball of fire. His fingernails bit into his palms. Sweat beaded out on his forehead, dampened his scalp at the hair line. He had an insane desire to grab Corcoran by the neck and strangle him until his face turned blue.

Sober reflection softened the anger a little. It wasn't entirely Corcoran's fault. He was slated for a much bigger job. Firing Dan was merely looking out for his own interests. If the higher-up heard nasty reports about the Keen Kleaner sales force, Corcoran might get the axe and be held responsible.

Smoking was strictly taboo any place in the office. No longer caring about rules. Dan fired up a cigarette, inhaled and blew the smoke directly into his boss's face. He had nothing to worry about. He was canned. Let Corcoran and all his crew go swing on the garden gate. There were other cleaner companies. Dan figured that if he could soil Keen Kleaners, he could sell the others.

He knew the weaknesses of the merchandise he was peddling. It had plenty of faults. He could play those up with a competitor's machine. And if Norton was made the new branch manager, Dan could take so much business away from him he'd be frothing at the mouth.

Corcoran's face was the colour of the Russian flag. Then the colour faded out and turned dead white. He began to choke up and his grey eyes became flakes of chipped ice.

'Damn you, Slick!' he roared. He climbed half out of his seat and shook his fist at Dan's smugly smiling face. 'You were the best damned salesman on the force. Why in hell couldn't you keep your nose clean? You had my job in a walk. Norton wasn't even close, no one else within spitting distance. Aw hell, what's the use?' he added as he sank back into his chair.

'Relax,' Dan told him with an easy grin. 'Don't lose your temper. It's bad for your blood-pressure. I kept my nose clean. I've been trying to side-step Norton ever since I joined this outfit. He's a jealous SOB. He wants to be top man and he doesn't care how he makes it or who he steps on doing it. I didn't start the fracas yesterday evening.'

Corcoran seemed willing enough to listen and Dan told him his side. He finished with, 'I should have knocked the bastard cold after he clubbed me silly with that beer bottle. The only reason I didn't was because I didn't want the company to get bad publicity. If you don't believe me, ask Eddie Goes. She was there and saw the whole thing. Ask the bartender or the waitress. Get the facts before you cut the ground out from under me.'

'Why didn't you report in this morning?' His voice was still cold, unfriendly, and rasping like a file on hard wood.

'I wanted to make that sale in Norton's territory,' Dan explained. 'The woman stood me up yesterday. I couldn't figure her out. She was either a dypso or a hot number, maybe a combination of both.'

'And a very good looking red-head.'

Dan nodded. 'Exotic is a better word. Also built, but a capacity like an elephant. She was at least three sheets in the wind when I rang the bell. If I'd guessed her condition I'd have remained outside. But I'd a tough day and I wanted a sale.'

'Did you have a drink with her?' Corcoran asked.

Dan saw no reason to withhold the truth. 'She offered me a highball and I took it. As a matter of fact we had a couple and fairly strong ones too. I demonstrated while she curled up on the davenport and listened.'

'How was she this morning?' Corcoran was beginning to show a lot of interest.

'I could have chinned myself on her breath when she opened the door.' Dan grinned and chuckled. 'You should see the dog. As big as a Shetland pony and as fierce looking, but all bark and no bite. Besides I'm a dog lover and they know it. We made fast friends on the veranda. His name is Bren, he's a brindle Great Dane.'

'Did you make a sale?'

'That's what I went there to do. That's what I did. Cash on the line and no trades. Everything in the deal including the bag, the spray outfit, the new floor waxer, plus an extra filter and bag which we'll mail to her.'

'You said the name was McGowan. Let me see the voucher?'

Dan handed him the voucher Eddie had prepared and which he hadn't cashed. Corcoran looked at it, switched on the intercom and told Eddie to bring in the original sales slip. The door opened a moment later. Eddie walked in, gave Dan a faintly questioning look and laid the slip on Corcoran's desk.

'Anything wrong, Boss?' she asked.

Corcoran waved her away with the abrupt reply, 'Nothing that you'd be interested in, Eddie. Just curious about the customer.'

Eddie vanished, the door closed and Corcoran stared up at Dan with an unreadable expression. He said finally, 'I think you have done the impossible, Dan. I don't suppose you have any idea who Mrs. McGowan is.'

'None whatsoever. Mrs. Clifton McGowan and her first name is Cleoney, Cleo for short. Red-headed and built, about thirty-one and been married to her husband for ten years. He's about six-foot-two, blue-eyed, and is in his early seventies according to Cleo.'

'Cleo?' Corcoran's eyebrows raised.

Dan reddened. 'She calls me Dan. She asked me to call her Cleo.'

He frowned. 'You must know that it's against all company rules to drink with prospects or customers.'

'Correct. So what? I'm fired. This paper proves it.' He waved the slip Corcoran had handed him. He was tired of the questions and he didn't think it was any of Corcoran's business who his customers were as long as they paid cash Somewhere in the back of his head was the thought that perhaps Corcoran intended to deliver the filter and the extra bag himself, so he could meet Mrs. McGowan.

'As for this job, Corcoran, you can stick it and shove it. I've got a damned good record with this outfit. I won't have any trouble working for one of your competitors. The minute they hear I'm finished here, they'll come looking for me.'

Dan ground the butt of his smoke into the carpet. 'So long sucker,' he said, 'And give all my love to that double-dealing, two-faced jerk, Tom Norton.'

'Damn it, sit down.' Corcoran cried with rising exasperation. When Dan somewhat reluctantly complied more out of curiosity than anything else, Corcoran said, 'Eddie told me all about last evening and she blamed Norton for starting it and praised you for not finishing it. And I have already checked with the bartender, the waitress, and a couple of other impartial witnesses. I was needling you, Slick. I wanted to find out what you'd say about Norton.'

Caught off guard by the sudden switch, Dan fumbled for another smoke. Corcoran stopped him with, 'You're still working here. When you're the manager you can change the rules and smoke your damned head off. But until you are, please do it outside. I'm allergic to the stuff.'

He started to smile and the smile broadened until it turned into a chuckle, then a laugh, and finally an exploding sound of mirth that made him pound his hands on the desk. When he finally recovered from that paroxysm he wiped his eyes and stared at Dan.

'I don't know whether to congratulate you or give you a gold medal, Slick. This morning you did something that is unheard of in the door-to-door sales game. You sold the big boss one of his own machines. By God, I can't believe it.'

Dan's eyes popped. 'You mean Clifton McGowan—'

'Chairman of the Board of Keen Kleaners and president of half a dozen other corporations as big. Got his fingers in a lot of pies. Wait till he hears this one. He could have had a hundred for free. This one he pays for. CASH, by God!' Corcoran subsided into silence, too deeply impressed to say anything more.

CHAPTER FIVE

D AN considered the information with gradual anxiety. Clifton
McGowan, the little he had seen of him, hadn't looked like
the type of man who would take kindly to having one of his
underlings call on his wife and sell her a machine that he could
obtain for free by calling any one of his offices. It was quite possible that McGowan might send down the word to give that fast-
talking salesman the bounce. And with the manager's job within
reach, Dan decided it would be just the kind of luck he could
expect.

'Do you know Mr. McGowan?' Dan asked with a worried
frown.

Corcoran shook his head. 'Never met the man, Slick. He
doesn't waste time calling on the branch managers. He has
men hired for that purpose, a job that I'll get when I leave
here. McGowan's a smart old fossil with a nose for the dollar.
According to all reports he's worth a couple of million or more.
If you're worried about your job, forget it. Did you get a sample
of that bad carpeting?'

Dan searched through his pockets until he found the square
of newspaper into which he had folded the pile of nap he had
emptied from his machine bag. 'It was like taking the hair off a
shedding dog. In a matter of seconds I made a bald spot as big
as a man's head. It's my guess someone used something stronger
than ordinary detergent to clean that carpet. I never saw moths
work that easily. She might sue, but I doubt it.'

Corcoran took the sample, dumped it into an envelope with the woman's name on it, filed it away in a drawer in his desk.

He closed the drawer and looked at Dan, his eyes friendly but cold. 'I'm leaving here on Monday, Slick. As of this morning you're the branch manager, subject to full approval of the main office of course. But I'm sure there won't be any trouble on that score. Especially after I tell them how you sold a machine for cash to the big boss's wife.'

'Do you have to do that?' Dan asked anxiously.

'I wouldn't miss it for the world,' Corcoran answered with a faint grin. 'It won't do you any harm. It'll clinch the job for you. Believe me I know. The boys upstairs love that sort of thing. There's an extra desk in the storage room. We'll move that in here and for the next day or two I'll work with you until you get accustomed to the routine.'

Corcoran stared at his new branch manager and seemed to read his mind. 'Don't let any past animosities cramp your style, Slick. I know you and Norton haven't gotten along too well and you've been sore at Eddie. Now it's up to you to be broad-minded. Norton's the second best salesman in the group. Eddies does her job efficiently and she knows the ropes. I'd give her a small raise after I'm gone. I don't want her to think it came from me. From now on all you're interested in is sales. Sales, sales and more sales. The head office will give you a quota to fill. Try and top it each month. They hand out a nice bonus when you do. Pick your men. Drive them hard. If they don't produce, get men who will.'

He gave Dan a patronizing smile. 'If you think this job is easier than the one you've had, you'll change your mind within a week. That much I'll guarantee. A salesman's day is finished when he turns in his orders and collects his commissions. Yours is never done. You'll find yourself sitting here night after night, all by your lonesome, trying to figure out how to make quotas and ways to beat them. The ones upstairs are never satisfied. They expect you to be superman. And don't forget there is plenty of room up there. A top-flight sales-manager is in good demand and they pay whopping salaries when you can produce. It's not too difficult to manufacture a vacuum cleaner, but they're no good to anyone sitting in a warehouse.'

He swiveled around and for a moment stared moodily out at the tall buildings and the distant tower of the City Hall, swiveled back again to face Dan. 'Sometimes I wish I'd remained a salesman. Sometimes I feel it hasn't been worth it. I've been a stranger to my family for the last five years. Most evenings the kids are tucked into bed and fast asleep when I get home, I get a kiss in the morning from my wife and away I go. That's the penalty, Slick. You're lucky you're a single man. And now I've got to move to Frisco. Drag the kids out of school, find a new home, and all new friends. My wife says she doesn't mind as long as I'm moving up in the world. Sometimes I wonder.'

His shoulders pulled back, the despairing look left his face and he said, 'Find that extra desk and get the janitor to move it in here. Tell Miss Macky I want her. I'll have her make a typewritten list of your new duties.'

Eddie was behind her desk when Dan came out of Corcoran's office. Dan felt like going over and telling her 'I told you so.' The stricken glance she gave him made him change his mind. Apparently she already knew, but he couldn't tell who she was feeling sorry for, Norton or herself.

She looked up from her work as his shadow fell across her desk. He couldn't tell her thoughts by the dark eyes. They were unreadable. But she said, 'You have my sincere congratulations, Mr. Slick.'

Memory flooded back and his eyes softened. 'I hope you mean that,' he told her. 'I'm going to need your help and the help of all the organization.'

She still refused to warm up. 'I'll do everything I can, Mr. Slick.'

By noon the word had reached the lowest echelon. Everyone began to polish the apple. When he had arrived that morning he'd been an outcast to most of them, some one beyond the pale. Now he was the boss.

Dan had a quick lunch in the cafe across the street, was back in the office within half an hour. By quitting time he was starting to appreciate what Corcoran had told him. There were reports to fill out, sales slips to check, vouchers to okay. The drudgery was taken care of by the office help, but the manager had to keep his fingers on the pulse of the business.

The next day was the same only worse. Dan's back was split in half from being cramped over a desk, his fingers were aching from pushing a pencil, his eyes bleary from looking at figures. But you didn't quit till the task was done if you were the manager. Late calls came in from salesmen who were still making demonstrations. You had to give them the right answers, the ones that would put more sales slips on your desk.

There were constant interruptions. The phone rang incessantly. At first it was a madhouse. It took a lot of time, a lot of guts, yet gradually routine came out of chaos and Dan learned how to organize his days. He had never been much good as a speaker. When he stood in front of his salesmen each morning, his throat clogged up, his voice broke, and sweat ran down his face like he was in a steam room. Corcoran suggested a small public address system.

It worked like a charm, Dan found, after he had used it a couple of times. The faces out front no longer frightened him.

They were just a bunch of men as anxious to earn money as he was. The apparatus in front of him, the small mike, could be turned up loud enough to send them screaming into the street with ruptured ear drums if he felt like it.

He had Miss Macky take notes of each speech. His little gems of wisdom, Dan called them. From those speeches he picked the meat and gradually developed a series of talks that anyone could give. The best of them he bound into a manual for the salesmen.

After Corcoran left the first thing Dan did was change the no smoking rule. The employees could smoke anytime, any place they chose to. It made a surprising difference in the amount of work turned out. They no longer had to sneak out to the washroom or the corridors for a quick inhale.

Norton never missed a meeting unless he had an early appointment. He was scrupulously polite to Dan, even bent over backwards to prove that he was doing what he could to help the new manager. Dan kept close tracks of his sales. There was no sluffing off. If any thing he was doing a little better. Dan knew one reason for that. Dan wasn't taking sales away from him.

Two weeks after he became manager Dan called Norton into the office. When he motioned him to a seat, Norton's eyes turned wary and watchful. He seemed unsure of himself and Dan knew that he was puzzled by the call.

To ease his anxieties, Dan told him he was doing a wonderful job and to keep up the good work. 'So far this month you're ahead of last. My job here depends on what you and the other men produce. I want to do everything I can to help you. I've had an idea kicking around in my head. I'd like to know what you think of it.'

'What kind of an idea?' Norton asked, still wary.

'I want to build a bigger sales force,' Dan told him. 'Split the territories into smaller units, make the men concentrate. I can't handle a bigger force by myself. I need an assistant manager.' He started to make a protest and Dan said quickly, 'Wait till I finish. I don't mean I want a man to sit on his butt here in the office all day like I do. The man I want is a better salesman than the others. Some one who can smooth over customer relations and knows all the answers. I can answer the phone and tell a man what to do, but I can't go out and show him. Get the idea?'

Norton shook his head and frowned. 'Frankly, I don't. If you're considering me for a job like that, I'm not interested. I can make more money in the field by myself. I know what your salary is, Mr. Slick.'

Dan realized that Norton had heard things from the cashier or even Eddie. But there were still some things that even the office help didn't know. Once a month the branch manager received a bonus from the head office. For each machine sold over his quota, the head office laid it on the line.

'You just think you know how much I make,' Dan told him with a supercilious smile that he couldn't help. 'And I don't intend to enlighten you other than to tell you this. My assistant will not only get his full commission on what he sells himself, he also gets an override on every sale made by the entire crew. It won't amount to much per machine, but at the end of the month it ought to mean at least three hundred extra and more.' Dan snubbed out the cigarette he had been staring and fired up a fresh one. 'I'm ambitious, Norton. I don't know how long Corcoran was here as manager. I don't care. All I know is that I'm going to produce. The sooner I prove that to the head office, the sooner they push me up another step. As my assistant you'd get first crack at my job. You lost out the last time to me, but that doesn't make you any worse a salesman.'

The wariness left Norton's face, and he began to smile. The idea seemed to please him. 'When do I start?' he asked.

'Next Monday,' Dan told him pleased with his own perspicacity. Norton was a better man to have on his side than against him. He stood up and stuck out his hand. 'Friends?' he asked with a warm grin.

Norton gripped his hand and said. 'I misjudged you, Mr. Slick. It was damned white of you to remember me. I won't let you down. And I won't be satisfied till we double Corcoran's last quota.'

That night for the first time since he had been appointed manager, Dan rode the elevator to the ground floor with Eddie in front of him. He was close enough to catch the scent of her unbelievably dark hair and see the small tendrils that curled at the nape of her neck. It looked as if it had been freshly washed and set that day.

The elevator touched the first floor and began to empty. Dan reached the revolving doors behind Eddie. It was not only raining, it was coming down in a steady downpour that would wet anything through that wasn't well protected with oilskins or a plastic raincoat. Eddie apparently had neither. She stopped under the awning that ran to the curb and looked anxiously up and down the street for a taxi. There wasn't an empty one in sight.

'Wet, isn't it?' Dan remarked as he came up to stand beside her. 'Can I give you a lift?'

She gave him the briefest of looks. 'Where is your car?'

'In the parking lot.'

'By the time I reached it I'd be as wet as I would if I waited for the bus on the corner.'

'Wrong again,' he answered. 'You wait here, I'll bring the car up.'

'I thought chivalry was dead,' she sneered. 'However, the prospect of ruining my shoes is worse than the thought of accepting your hospitality. I agree.'

Ten minutes later Dan drove up, stopped in front of the building's entrance. She opened the door, climbed in quickly, shook the rain off her head as she shut the door. Dan was wetter than he had expected to be. He had mistaken a large puddle for just another bit of shining macadam. He turned on the heater. The water swished around in his shoes as he braked frequently on the wet streets.

Eddie stayed huddled over in her corner, silently watching the wipers sweeping back and forth, the rain-soaked pedestrians hurrying for shelter, the rain streaming across the windshield. She could hear the hum of tires on wet macadam, the steady pulsating sound of the motor.

Dan drew up in front of her building. Before he could get out to help her, she had the door open and one foot on the curb. 'Thanks for the lift,' she said with cool indifference.

'The pleasure is all mine,' he told her with a wry smile, 'only you weren't very good company. If I didn't have to leave so early I'd come for you in the morning. According to the newscast this rain is due to last for at least three days.'

Her winged eyebrows made arches above her dark expressionless eyes. 'I heard your feet swishing around in your shoes. Would you care to accept my hospitality long enough to dry them a little?' She remained where she was, poised to leave quickly, but waiting for his response.

He answered her by shutting off the ignition and moving quickly around to her side. Afterwards they rode the elevator together to the top floor. She unlocked the door to her apartment, opened it, stepped inside. When he was in, she closed it and stood with her back to it, staring up at him. The look in her eyes moved his body closer to her without any concious effort. He slid his hand round her waist, placing his palm against the small of her back. When he exerted a little pressure she came to him willingly enough.

'Let's quit playing childish games, Eddie,' he suggested. 'I'm nuts about you. Have been ever since our first date.'

'And last,' she added in faint malice. Her eyes were deep, dark pools of loneliness. 'You've had an odd way of showing it. If you really mean that, Dan, tell me again.'

He told her in a better way.

Then, as far as Dan was concerned, the world became a dark and torturous void of emptiness.

CHAPTER SIX

AN engine from the Santa Fe switch yards hooted eerily. A horn barked an angry warning from the street. Rain beat a steady tattoo on the roof above the apartment. Dan opened his eyes, tried to make them focus on something familiar, closed them again tight, then reopened them.

He knew he was on his back. He could smell the dust in the carpet and the center fixture in the ceiling stared back at him like a huge blind eye of a dead monster. His hands could feel pieces of broken pottery near him and he groaned involuntarily.

The sound brought other objects into his vision, the particular one, Eddie, who stood well out of reach with a small automatic in her hand, her dark eyes venomous with dislike.

'If you can walk,' she told him, biting off each word angrily, 'get your legs under you and scram. If you don't get out of here in a hurry I'll call the police.'

Dan's head was revolving like a carousel and his head ached in a thousand places. The immediate past was a complete blank. He looked at her with a puzzled frown, unable to understand either the gun she menaced him with or the pieces of pottery on the floor beside him.

'Why did you hit me, Eddie?' he asked plaintively.

'Don't try and play cute with me,' she sneered. I happen to be fond of my ribs. They are the only set I have. If I hadn't hit you with the lamp you'd have broken me in half. I don't care for big lugs with iron muscles. And you owe me for one lamp. Now suppose you gather yourself together, get off my floor and get out of here.'

It came back to him then, the clap of thunder, his own involuntary muscular reaction. He tried to explain as he pulled himself erect. He'd spent four years in the Navy, the last two as a Frogman. His buddy had been blown into eternity by the premature explosion of an under-water demolition charge. Dan had been lucky. The dead man had acted as a buffer. He'd spent eight months in the Veterans' Hospital at Long Beach. They called it combat fatigue. The backfire of a truck could send him into a tailspin.

They had finally discharged him as cured. To all intents he was, but once in a great while something like that clap of thunder would set him off again.

'That was one of those times, Eddie. Honest, honey. I wouldn't hurt you for the world. You were just unlucky enough to be in my arms when it happened.'

She looked sceptical. She wanted to believe. He could tell that by the look in her eyes. She did finally. She helped him to the davenport, got a cold cloth to wipe the blood off his face. She lit a smoke for him, helped him remove his soaked shoes and sox, got him a towel to dry his feet. She took the shoes and sox out into the kitchen and placed them on the oven door. She made him a highball and vanished back into the kitchen to put on the coffee maker.

Afterwards they talked of the new job and she thanked him for the raise. He told her about what he had offered Norton. She liked his generosity in forgetting their old dislikes.

'It wasn't because of that,' he shrugged. 'I don't think I'll ever learn to like him. But Norton can increase business in that kind of a spot. It will keep his nose to the grindstone and give me a little time to get out in the field occasionally so I can keep my hand in. How about having dinner with me, honey?'

Tonight?'

She was on the far end of the davenport, too far for him to reach if he had another attack. She was poised like a bird, ready to take flight at a moment's notice.

There were still occasional flashes of lightning, but no thunder and the storm seemed to have lessened as it moved southeast. The tattoo had diminished on the roof.

'Why not?' he asked. 'I can stand damp shoes and sox if you can. It would be like old times.'

'I'm too tired and my ribs ache.' She shook her head. She managed a tired smile that took the sting out of her refusal. 'You don't realize what a bone-crusher you can be, Dan. Maybe the rain's about over temporarily, but I like my rainy nights at home. Sorry, Dan. Some other time.'

She brought back his shoes and sox. He got to his feet. She did too, watching him warily. He saw the fear in her eyes and he said, 'Relax, honey. It won't happen again. I promise.'

Dan got a peck for a good night kiss, no more.

The next night he drove her home again, picked her up in the morning. Nothing more was said about the bone-crushing incident although he was sure she hadn't forgotten it. He didn't get kissed as frequently as he wished and the kisses were apt to be short. She was still fearful of his strength.

There were lots of nights when he couldn't take her home. He had to remain for late calls or paper work. But even when he didn't take her home, he managed to see her later, have dinner with her, or take her to a late show.

Dan was sure that he had found the right woman. He was in love, deeply, sincerely, and desperately. Many times he suggested marriage. She wanted no part of holy wedlock. At least not yet. Her reasons were valid enough.

'I'm happier with you than I am with any one else. I look forward to our evenings together. But let's forget about marriage for the present. You have a job to do. Some day you'll be district manager. When that time comes you may have different ideas about me. After all I'm just a nobody. I've very little education. A man in the top spot needs a wife with looks and brains.'

'You've got both,' he argued. 'And I won't change.'

The call came the next morning around ten. It was for Dan personally. The operator had tried to switch the call to Norton. It was Mrs. McGowan and she wished to talk to Mr. Slick, no one else. Dan recognized the husky overtones the moment she spoke. She was having a little trouble using the de-mother. Would he mind awfully coming to the house? She remembered that he had promised to give her machine his personal attention. If possible she would like him to be there not later than eleven.

Dan was up to his ears in work. It was time for the monthly report, a dozen other tasks that couldn't wait. But Cleo McGowan was the big boss's wife. If she wanted the general manager himself to fly to her from Pittsburg, she could have him.

Everyone in the office had heard how he had sold a cleaner to the boss's wife. Now they knew she had called and demanded the manager himself to do repair work. If they had dared, they'd have given him the big raspberry as he left.

Eddie was the only one who looked mad. 'I suppose you're invited for lunch,' she remarked.

Dan grinned at her. 'If it's offered I'll accept. She's a dish, Eddie. Like I told you. A deep-dish apple pie topped with thick whipped cream.

'Don't forget the cherry,' she told him acidly.

He chuckled. 'Oh, you mean the red hair. Jealous, honey?'

'You're damned right,' she hissed back. 'I've never seen that hussy, but I don't trust her any further than I can kick the City Hall. You watch your step, you big lug. A frail like that can be poison. I know. It was one like that who latched on to my first husband.'

'I don't think you have anything like that to worry about,' he told her. 'She would hardly trade a multimillionaire for a branch manager. This call is strictly business. It might help the next step up the ladder. I'd like to get to know the old man himself. Who knows, he might like my looks.'

'That's why she called.'

'Dig that deeper. I don't get you.'

'She likes your looks, stupid,' Eddie leered.

Dan laughed. 'Not this mug, honey. See you later.'

It was a good half hour's drive to Brentwood and all the way he wondered. He couldn't imagine anyone with Cleo McGowan's class going for him. She was the kind who liked money, plenty of it. She might go off the deep end when she was full of fire-water, but not when she had time to consider what she already had.

For the first time as he walked up the curving driveway from the gateway to the house, he took more notice of the landscaping. The house covered the entire front of the wide lot and what wasn't covered by it, had ornamental red tile fencing with only a single gate beyond the three car garage. The drapes had been drawn the last time he had been inside and he hadn't been able to see what kind of a yard or patio they had, but he'd have been willing to bet there would be a swimming pool someplace.

A maid answered his ring. Dan handed her his card, told her that he had an appointment to either repair the de-mother or to show them how to use it. The maid seemed a little sceptical, but she stood to one side and let him enter. Once he was inside, she motioned him into the room where he had demonstrated before and told him that she would call Mrs. McGowan.

She was middle-aged, flat-footed, and grey-haired. She looked as if she might be a combination cook and housekeeper. She gave Dan a single glance that told him without question that she didn't approve of his looks.

Dan sat down. Time moved along on sluggish legs and he glanced at his wristwatch, surprised to discover that only ten minutes had passed since his arrival. He began to wonder what Cleo McGowan would appear in this time. The first time it had been a peasant skirt and off-the-shoulder blouse. The second time it had been an equally exotic looking house dress. Perhaps this time it would be in snug-fitting sweater and tapering tore-ador pants. No matter what she wore, he felt sure she'd look good to him.

She caught him flat-footed. He heard her voice from the yard, then suddenly she parted the drapes that hung across the windows from wall to wall and stepped into the room from the patio. For a brief moment he was numb with astonishment. Except for the gold sandals he had thought she was completely unclothed. She wasn't. What he had thought was bare skin was a latex suit that was almost the exact color of her skin and hugged her slim body. But what unnerved him even more was her hair. It was no longer copper-toned and long. It was cut into short curls that made a halo around her face and it was platinum white.

The same topaz eyes regarded Dan with faint amusement. 'Good morning, Dan. I forgot I told you to be here not later than eleven. I was sun-bathing and I lost track of the time. I'll have Nellie bring in the cleaner. You can explain to her what is wrong or how you operate the de-mother. I'm afraid I wasn't listening very carefully when you sold it to me.' Her voice lifted a full tone. 'Nellie!'

The maid reappeared and Mrs. McGowan gave her instructions to bring the machine with its attachments into the living room. After she had left, she turned back to Dan. 'If you'll excuse me, Dan. I'm not very efficient with anything mechanical. Nellie does that. But after you're finished, come into the patio. I'd like to talk with you.'

Up until that time Dan had been too flustered to even greet her. Now he managed to mumble a few words, all of which sounded inane to him and he was glad when she parted the drapes and vanished and the maid returned.

Inside of ten minutes he had attached the vaporizer, filled it with moth crystals and attached it to the hose and the hose to the bag. Nellie caught on quickly, insisted she could operate it without any further trouble and opened the drapes so that he could step into the patio.

'I believe you will find Mrs. McGowan down by the pool. Sir,' she told him.

The yard was much larger than Dan had expected because the lot was very deep. There was a white stucco and frame bath house facing a larger than average kidney-shaped pool. There was a cement supported diving board at one end together with a chrome ladder. Around the flagstoned pool were chairs, chaise longues and pads for sunbathing. Mrs. McGowan was stretched out on one of these, her eyes covered with dark glasses.

Dan came down the walk and reached the pool side. She heard him and sat up smiling. 'Finished so quick?' she asked. 'Make yourself comfortable on one of the chaise if you like. I told Joseph to mix a pair of Planter's punches when he saw you were finished. He's exceedingly prompt. He should be here any moment. I do hope you like rum drinks. In this kind of weather they're my favourites.'

He hadn't been tongue-tied when he had sold her the machine. Now he was. She was so much more glamorous than she had been. Along with the clothes was a model's figure to go with it. The legs were long and beautifully formed. Dan felt sure that if she had been alive when the Follies were popular, Ziegfeld would have picked her at first glance.

The new hair do and color mysteriously changed her entire personality. Where before she had seemed hot-blooded and unpredictable, now she appeared cool and self possessed. Either she had laid off the booze for the time being or she was carrying it better than she did before. There was no sign of it in the clear eyes, none in the tones of her voice.

Suddenly she giggled. It was the first thing that seemed normal to Dan and he grinned down at her, not sure of what she found that was so amusing, but willing to share it with her.

'You're a very strange man, Dan,' she explained with unexpected soberness. 'I should have thanked you a long time ago for what you did for me that morning. I am deeply ashamed and you were a perfect gentleman. Some men might have taken advantage of my condition. I think that's one reason I like you so much.'

'You had an asthmatic attack,' he answered. 'And you were a good prospect for a sale.'

'And the big boss's wife,' she chimed in impishly.

'That I didn't know when I punched the bell. Corcoran didn't tell me until after I had made the sale. You could have knocked me loopy with a paper match stick when I heard. I was scared stiff. Your husband could have a carload of cleaners for free. Just why did you buy that one from me?' he added curiously. Apparently she had known it all the time.

'Let's just say I liked your looks. I think I told you the first time you called that I was a very lonely woman.'

'I didn't think you remembered.'

The butler in black trousers and a white coat appeared with a tray and two tall glasses which he silently distributed. He asked if there was anything else that Madame wished. She shook her head and he disappeared as unobtrusively as he had arrived.

Dan got no more than a cursory look at the man. He guessed he was about Dan's own age, somewhere in his early thirties and the accent was as phoney as a nine dollar bill.

She took a sip of her drink, placed it on the concrete and leaned back on her hands, with her long legs stretched in front of her, the sandaled feet turning in.

'I'd had some bad news that day,' she explained simply. 'Both my Nellie and Joseph were off and I was lonely as hell. I tried to drown my loneliness with the bottle. You happened in at the crucial moment. I was never so glad to see anyone in my life. I could have kissed you.' She glanced at him slyly, watching for his reaction.

He was fast losing any embarrassment he had felt at first, but he wasn't losing sight of the fact that she was the big boss's wife. She was still a deep-dish apple pie topped with rich whipped cream, but she was not for the likes of Daniel Slick.

'It's against the rules for salesmen to kiss prospects, no matter how attractive they are,' he told her with a shrug. 'It's against the rules to accept a drink. Here I am breaking the rules. If you told your husband, he'd throw me out on my ear.'

This was his chance to perhaps meet the big Boss socially. Everything helped and he wanted that District Manager's job. He wanted more than that, but he knew it would have to wait. He could hardly expect to be a vice-president so quickly.

'You must have a very low opinion of me to suggest that I would inform my husband of some small infractions of the company rules. I told him this morning that I needed some one to explain the machine's use. He was the one who suggested that I call you.' She laughed softly. 'He's taken an awful lot of ribbing since you sold me one of his machines. He's come to the conclusion that you're a super-salesman. Would you like to meet him?'

Dan's heart began to pound and he said, 'Would I? That's a silly question, Mrs. McGowan. Of course I'd like to meet him. Someday I hope to be up there where he is.' Then a thought struck him that put a worried crease along his forehead. 'But would it be wise to meet him through you? He might get the wrong impression.'

Her lips drooped in a faint sneer. 'He's changed his mind about me having men friends. He's suggested that I'm too cooped up. Could you come for dinner tonight? Clifton won't be home until late, but you could stay and meet him then. I'd appreciate it terribly. I really would, Dan. And please call me Cleo.'

Dan accepted the invitation, but the moment he was back in his car, sober reflection made him regret the acceptance. He didn't know why, but some premonition of trouble rose in his thoughts to plague him. Getting too familiar with the Boss's wife could lead to some touchy entanglements.

CHAPTER SEVEN

EDDIE'S dark eyebrows raised in bewildered surprise when Dan walked into the office at just a few minutes after the noon hour.

'What no luncheon date? You must be slipping.'

'Cut and dried,' he told her. 'The maid listened. The luscious Madame McGowan was toasting her gorgeous body by the sapphire-swimming pool.'

'How do you know?' Eddie frowned and her eyes grew bright with quick jealousy.

'We had a chat after the demonstration,' Dan grinned, recognizing the jaundiced look and loving it. 'She's going to introduce me to the old man himself.'

'She's a fraud, Dan. Watch your step. Never trust a red-head.'

'Tain't red no longer, honey. It's that new shade so many of the girls are sporting. I think they call it platinum.'

'I knew it came out of a bottle.' She frowned up at him. 'It takes hours to bleach hair to that shade, especially when you have a brunette base.'

'On her it looks good,' he said, needling her anxiety. 'What a dish! I wonder how an old geezer like McGowan holds on to something like that.'

'Simple. The answer is money, my friend. That type will sell their souls for a diamond bracelet and a wagon load of mink.'

The office was empty except for Eddie. Dan leaned over and kissed her on the forehead. 'She's not my type, honey. I still like the true brunettes. And you're dead right. She's still just another Hollywood blonde. As soon as Macky gets back, give me a buzz on the intercom. We'll go out to lunch.'

He had no more than a half hour to work on his papers when the intercom buzzed. Miss Macky was back at the switchboard. Eddie was ready any time he was.

As far as Dan was concerned it was a most satisfying meal and an hour and a half well spent. Eddie didn't have the appeal of the fascinating Mrs. McGowan, but she was a better buy in spite of it. She was not so much tinsel and glitter. She was for real. Dan was in love with her. So much so that he asked her again to marry him. He had the feeling that he'd be a good deal safer and more apt to side-step entangling alliances if he had a wife.

Eddie was starry-eyed at the proposal, but she still refused to say yes. 'There's plenty of time, Dan darling, for us to make up our minds. You're on your way up. I want to be sure and so do you that we're right for each other.'

She could be very stubborn when she felt like it. Dan didn't try to break down her defences. He was sure that his love for Eddie would act as a shield. Cleo was gorgeous, but not for a poor cleaner salesman. The only cloud on their luncheon came when Dan told her that he had been invited to the McGowan's for dinner that evening.

'She doesn't waste any time,' Eddie almost snarled. 'I'll say that much for her. I suppose this is the old man's night to play poker with the boys.'

Dan didn't tell her the truth. He told her that McGowan would be there as far as he knew and that the whole object of the invitation was for him to meet the head of Keen Kleaners.

Eddie was still burning when they returned to the office. Dan, decided she was more scared than jealous, scared and worried that some other woman might cut in on her time. His reassurances did no good and he gave up trying and fell to work, plowing through his reports with a vengeance and trying to clean up as much as possible before quitting time. He worked so fast and furiously he had the entire office force jittery.

He drove Eddie to her apartment building, kissed her good night, and for a long moment held her in his arms while he tried again to reassure her. He felt as if he was about to take a trip around the world instead of one to Brentwood. She was as full of reasons why he should not go to McGowan's as a pomegranate is full of seeds.

He told her firmly. 'Honey, I'm not off to battle with a monster. Mrs. McGowan may be a fraudulent frail and it's quite possible she has ulterior motives that a dumb ox like me can't discern, but so what? I don't think she has murder on her mind? As for me being carried away by her classy-chassis, there is nothing wrong with the one I'm holding in my arms, I love you, sweetheart. Nothing's going to change that. Marry me, dammit. Put a halter around my neck and bridle too. I gentle real easy.'

She wanted no part of that yet. Dan watched her vanish into the elevator, then returned to his car. He had no dinner clothes and he wasn't sure whether or not they were indicated. He settled for his best, a dark blue flannel, a white shirt and a tie that didn't leap out and slap you in the face.

Promptly at six thirty he presented himself at the McGowan home Joseph bowed him in. Joseph was in a monkey suit with a red cummerbund, a bow tie and kerchief to match.

'Mr. McGowan sends his regrets, Mr. Slick,' he announced. 'He will not be home until a very late hour.'

Dan wondered if it was premeditated or just happenstance. He didn't have much time to think about it. He was scarcely ushered into the living room when the chimes sounded again. Joseph opened the door and a slightly built, rather handsome but effeminate looking man entered. Like Joseph he was in a white dinner coat only with an embroidered gold cummerbund, a tie and kerchief to match. Joseph's shirt was plain. The newcomer's was lace-frilled in three rows from neck to belt line.

Joseph did the honours. 'Mr. Daniel Slick, may I present Mr. Carl Mabee. Mr. Mabee, Mr. Slick.' He bowed, moved over to the small bar that had been brought out of the wall from its hidden receptacle, and asked what the gentlemen preferred.

Mabee took a Scotch over the rocks, Dan said he'd like a dry Martini. He felt as helpless as a violet in the subway rush. He had seen many of the breed and the few he had seen, he'd carefully avoided, but if Mabee wasn't a strange type, he was certainly a more than reasonable facsimile of one.

To make it more embarrassing, Mabee seemed to like his looks. 'I've heard of you, Mr. Slick. Cleo told me how you sold the Emperor one of his own cleaners. It was delightful. Everyone in the company got a good laugh out of it.'

'Everyone but Mr. McGowan I imagine,' Dan answered with a faint smile. 'You work for the company, Mr. Mabee?'

Mabee shook his head. 'Only indirectly. I am Mr. McGowan's personal attorney. Gracious! Here comes Cleo now. Isn't she simply too gorgeous for words?'

Dan had to admit that she was all of that and then some. The evening gown was reasonably high in the front but cut almost to her waist in the back. It was shimmering crimson satin and fitted her closely. Dan wasn't sure what held it up. It hugged every curve no matter which way she turned or moved. The only jewels were an emerald and diamond bracelet, a huge square cut emerald that exploded from her engagement finger and a plain platinum wedding ring.

Mabee kissed the hand she extended. Dan just had the strength to grasp it once and drop it. But that hand didn't leave him for long. It came back to rest on his shoulder and even through the flannel of his shirt he could feel the heat of it, like a warm iron.

'I'm so delighted you could make it, Dan', she told him with a warmth that made his blood pound through his veins. 'And I'm sorry that Clifton won't be here. It seems there is some kind of a merger in the making Perhaps Carl can give you the details although I'm not sure they are ready for publication.'

'Hush, hush,' Mabee chimed in. 'You look simply ravishing, Cleo. That dress. It's adorable and so becoming. It makes me so sad when I see a woman in such gorgeous raiment.'

'Don't know why it should,' Dan remarked. 'Women look better in plumage than men.'

'But of course,' Mabee agreed. 'Though I often wished that I lived in the time of Louis the 14th. They dressed so divinely then. Silks and satins, gorgeous powdered wigs. In those days the men were as beautifully turned out as the women.'

Cleo gave Dan a furtive glance to catch his reaction to her other guest. Dan tried to keep a poker face. There was no longer any doubt in his mind as to Mabee. He was definitely on the strange side. He wondered why his hostess had invited him.

The conversation turned to music, the Symphony Orchestra that was playing in town that month. Dan accepted another Martini from Joseph who appeared and vanished like a jack-in-the-box. Once again he was out in the cold. He knew nothing about music and less about the symphony orchestra.

He wouldn't have called the dinner a howling success. Mabee monopolized the conversation and he and Cleo seemed to have some common bond of friendship that Dan couldn't analyze. He was sure she was a normal and healthy female. He couldn't begin to understand why she found Mabee so attractive.

After the meal was over they had a demi-tasse in the living room, with the French doors open and the pool and the patio artfully illuminated with reflected and hidden lights of various shades. It was definitely a spot for romance.

Dan excused himself to go to the wash room and upon his return he caught his hostess and the attorney in an argument which they broke off the moment he appeared. He'd heard his name mentioned and he knew intuitively that they had been talking about him. This made him even more uncomfortable and he wished that he could find some excuse to leave.

That desire was taken out of his hands by Mabee's announcement that he had a very important appointment with a client and would have to leave. He kissed his hostess's hand in farewell, offered his to Dan with the polite statement that he was delighted to meet him. If Dan had any doubts previously as to Mabee, the hot clamminess of the attorney's palm and fingers settled it.

After Mabee had gone, Cleo took a white woollen stole from the hall closet and suggested to Dan that they sit on the terrace. The chaise longue she picked out to relax upon was a double one of wicker and black iron and wide enough for at least three people to lie on either prone, if they wished, or partially upright. She ordered Joseph to bring ice, highball glasses, a bottle of soda and the Amontillado decanter of brandy.

After she had arranged herself in the way she wished, she told Dan to sit beside her. Joseph reappeared with the liquor, placed it on a side table, then unobtrusively vanished. Dan wondered if the man was wearing rubber or crepe-soled shoes. He just seemed to appear and disappear not only in the twinkling of an eye, but without any sound.

Dan hadn't realized that he was staring at her until she asked softly, 'Will I do, Dan?' The topaz eyes gleamed. He pulled his mind back. Her laugh was low and vibrant. 'You looked as if you were off in the wide blue yonder. What did you think of Carl?'

'Okay, I guess, for those who like that type.'

She giggled. At that moment Joseph appeared in his customary mysterious manner and announced that he and the maid were ready to leave if Mrs. McGowan had no objections. She waved him away and Dan asked if they didn't live on the premises.

'We have no servants' quarters,' she told him. 'Clifton doesn't like to have them under his feet when he wants to be alone. They both come early, at least early enough to prepare his breakfast and to do the housework. But for heaven's sake, let's not talk about such mundane things as servants. I want to know you better, Dan. Where do you come from? What have you done? Where have you been? You look to me like a man who's seen a great deal of life.'

Dan grinned. 'Lived long enough to appreciate a lovely woman when I meet her. There's an old song a buddy of mine wrote while I was in the Navy that went, "Gee but it's tough to fall in love with somebody who can never belong to you." That sort of covers my feelings.'

'You haven't known me long enough to fall in love with me,' she protested, but with a pleased smile. Her warm hand reached out and came to rest on his leg. The exotic scent she wore made his mouth dry.

He had seen the same look in her eyes the first day he had called to make a demonstration. He'd been afraid of her then; afraid even to reach out and see if she would resist his advances. He no longer was. This was the big Boss's wife, but the wife wanted to play games, and she had volunteered to introduce him to her husband. That made the set-up different, to his way of thinking. Sure, he loved Eddie, he told himself, but there was no harm in making something as lovely as Cleo McGowan contented.

'I could very easily have fallen in love with you the first time I met you,' he told her. 'When you opened the door in the peasant outfit, you could have bowled me over with a slight breeze. I was completely fascinated.'

'But you didn't,' she countered.

Dan turned enough so that he could look at her fully, their bodies almost touching. 'That day I was a salesman, Mrs. McGowan.'

She interrupted him quickly with, 'The name is Cleo, Dan.'

He nodded and continued. 'Having seen you I had to relegate you into the background in order to concentrate. I'd had a bad day. Just the sight of you gave me a lift and I wanted to make at least one sale.'

'But you couldn't quite make it, could you?'

He knew she was ribbing him and he didn't care in the least, 'I don't think any red-blooded man could. I had to get out in a hurry or forget my manners and all the company rules,'

'Is it against the company rules to kiss a prospect?' she asked with a giggle.

'Definitely,' he assured her. 'It's also against the rules to drink with one, which I did with you. Frankly, when I ran out, I was afraid you might call the office and snitch on me. If you had I'd have lost my job. Corcoran was manager then and he was a tough baby and a stickler for the rules. Then the next time I saw you, I thought you were an uncooked length of spaghetti. You really shocked me that time until I discovered it was a bathing suit.'

Her lips parted in a hearty laugh. 'I call that suit my shocker. When Nellie told me there was a man awaiting an appointment I honestly never gave it a thought. As a matter of fact I'd forgotten I'd called for service. I thought you were some one else.'

Carl Mabee, Dan thought instantly.

She refilled her glass and his, handed it to him and moved over a little closer so that their shoulders touched. He could feel the warmth of her through the light-weight flannel.

'You still haven't told me anything about yourself,' she prodded.

Dan told her where he was born and all about his uncle Dan who had raised him, the extent of his education and his four years in the Navy.

'I think I'd like to have known your Uncle Dan,' she conceded. 'He sounds like a very virile and interesting individual. I'd guess that you must favor him. You're the type of man that most women prefer.

'What about you?' he asked. 'Born to the manor I suspect. Raised in the lap of luxury.'

She laughed heartily. 'You're a rotten judge of females, Dan. I was practically born in the gutter. I managed one year of high school before I had to go to work. Had a good figure and the looks so I was soon a striptease artist. The pay was bettter than anything else and you'd be surprised the nice men who come around and buy your meals and clothes if you do your part. That's how I met Clifton. His wife had died and he was lonely. I filled the bill for a time. Actually, Dan, I'm just a big phoney. All that talk tonight about the symphony was a lot of hogwash. I can't carry a tune and I don't know the first thing about highbrow music.'

With no advance warning she turned suddenly and let herself fall across his knees. The glass fell to the flagstone terrace, bounced once and tinkled as it cracked and split apart. She paid no attention to it. She already had one arm around Dan's neck and she was by sheer force, bringing his face down while she lifted hers.

Dan didn't have time to set his drink down. And he couldn't operate satisfactorily with one hand. He thought, to hell with the glass. If she could drop hers and let it break he could do the same with his. He scarcely heard it strike and crash. Her lips were against his, he had one arm around her back supporting her, the other on her leg.

Eddie was relegated into the background. What he had in his arms was something extra special, a woman who could do him a lot of good if he strung along and made her happy. At the moment that was all that counted. He only hoped her husband didn't decide to come home early.

CHAPTER EIGHT

DAN had never experienced or known a woman quite like Cleo McGowan. When she wanted something she didn't spend a lot of time beating around the bush. He could see his wrist watch and it surprised him to note that it was less than twenty minutes since Carl Mabee had left.

As if she guessed that he was looking at his watch, she moved tighter against him.

The eerie wail of a siren lifting over the amazing stillness of the patio broke the spell. She pushed herself away from Dan, stared at him a long moment, then with a sudden impulsion she squealed, 'I know what we'll do now. We'll go swimming, darling. The pool is heated. Clifton keeps it at around eighty-five degrees. It's just right for a night like this. You'll find a pair of trunks in the bath house. The light switch is on your right as you go in. Hurry,' she urged. 'We haven't got all night. Clifton is due home later. I want to have all the fun I can with you before he arrives,'

She was like a dryad scurrying for the house. The colored lights turned the crimson material of her dress into a deep purple. It reflected from the golden-tanned skin of her back and made the off-white platinum hair shine like a halo around her head.

Somewhat wearily Dan climbed to his feet, heard the crunch of glass as he stepped on it, and took the time to sweep it under the chaise longue with his shoe. His chest was damp with perspiration.

He had no trouble finding the light switch or the trunks and he disrobed quickly, anxious to feel the touch of the cool water. Eighty five degrees seemed like rather a high heat to keep the water in a swimming pool, but then he told himself that McGowan was an old man. He would naturally dislike the first touch of anything much colder.

He stepped out of the bath house and walked to the pool. The light at the deep end refracted as it spun through the blue water. The diving board was at the other end. It was easier to swim than to walk to it. He plunged in, making his dive flat to avoid the shallowness. In a few strokes he reached the ladder and climbed out.

After the warmness of the pool, the air seemed colder than an Irishman's nose the night he was buried. Dan went back in, swam the length of the pool, and back and hung to the coping, wishing that he had a cigarette.

Cleo came out of the house in the same suit he had seen her in before. It was difficult to tell where the skin and the material met. In the patio lights she was a dryad again. She wore no bathing cap. In one hand she carried a pack of cigarettes and a package of paper matches. She placed these on the tile coping within reach of his hand.

'How's the water, darling?' She stood looking down at him, the expression in her eyes unreadable.

'Elegant,' he answered. He reached for a cigarette, managed to light it in spite of his wet hands.

'Why didn't you bring out a towel?' she asked in surprise. 'There's a whole stack of clean ones in the bath house.'

'This is okay for now', he told her. 'A woman with your looks shouldn't bother with clothes. You ought to be living on a south sea island.'

She pirouetted in front of him, stopped and giggled. 'I know you men. That's all you ever think about.'

'What else is there that's worth thinking about when a lovely female is around? I'm normal, my sweet. I enjoy a woman's presence as much as the average man. Not like Mabee, perhaps.' He couldn't help adding that and she laughed.

That's a good sign, darling. You're jealous.'

'Jealous as hell', he assured her. 'My tough luck you're married. We'd make a helluva team, you and me. With your husband's money and my ideas, we could go places and really enjoy life. That's the trouble these days. Between taxes and the high cost of living, there's not much you can do to lay away for your old age. It's hard to make it so you can still enjoy it while you're young.'

'You talk too much.'

She stepped off the coping into the water, went to the tile bottom of the pool, pushed herself back to the surface so that she was facing Dan and close enough for him to touch.

She asked for a cigarette. He took one from the pack, lit it and handed it to her. She drew the smoke deep into her lungs, exhaled slowly through her lips. Tastes good', she said. Suddenly she tossed the unfinished cigarette to the grass. 'To hell with smoking, Kiss me, darling.'

He tossed his butt over the side of the pool, hung on to the coping with one hand and reached for her. She moved in close.

Time passed. Then:

'What did you hear?' He was worried. If the big boss should come home earlier than expected and find him in such a position with his wife, he'd be apt to catch a slug through his guts as well as lose that new manager's job.

'I thought I heard the front door open', she shrugged nonchalantly 'Now don't get scared and run away.'

'I couldn't run away if I wished.' He gave her a wry smile and before she could try anything new, he pushed away from the pool's end and swam to the shallow part.

She was as good as any of the finny family when she had the desire. She came towards him in a fast crawl with the form of an Olympic star. When she had almost reached him, he took off in the opposite direction. She made an about face and caught him at the other end of the pool. She pushed herself out of the water, surprised him off guard, and came down on top of his head. The next thing he knew he was gasping for air, and fighting to reach the surface.

She released her hold, he caught his breath and shook the water out of his eyes. She was hanging to the coping and grinning at him with faint malice.

'You couldn't swim away either, darling,' she giggled.

He ducked suddenly and came up under her, tossing her over his shoulders. She went all the way to the bottom and stayed there for what seemed like hours. Suddenly scared he dived down, gripped her by her suit, hauled her back to the surface. Her eyes were closed and she lay limp in his arms.

Thoroughly frightened now he hauled her out of the pool, stretched her on the flagstone and began to give her artificial respiration. She turned her head and looked up at him, giggling like a child who has been caught stealing from the cooky jar.

'You're breaking my back,' she told him. 'Just in case you don't realize it. I just wanted to see what you'd do. Get some of those big towels out of the bath house. I think I've had enough swimming for one night. It's turning chilly.'

The towels were terry cloth and as big as bed sheets. He wrapped one around her, one around himself and they returned to the living room. She turned up the thermostat while he retrieved the liquor and glasses from the patio. She fluffed up her light hair, ran a comb through it, applied lipstick and a touch of makeup.

She drank two brandies neat, and still wrapped in the towel, draped herself across Dan's lap, with one arm around his shoulders, with another brandy in her fist. He'd forgotten all about the big boss and that Cleo was the boss's wife. She was too lucious a morsel to be overlooked and too determined not to be.

Two brandies and he began to feel good. The look in her eyes affected him even more deeply than the Amontillado brandies. He hadn't thought of Eddie and how her lips felt since his first kiss with Cleo. It was as if some one had erased everything in his memory: erased everything except the presence of the woman in his arms.

With a sudden hoarseness that he couldn't control he cried out, 'Damnit, Cleo. What in hell do you think I am? He knew he couldn't continue much longer without going out of his mind. 'Let's quit this lallygagging. I'm crazy about you.'

She closed his mouth with hers and her hand moved. No longer caring, he reached for her. His hands touched her and froze there. Someone was at the front door. He had distinctly heard the sound of a key being inserted into a lock.

He didn't wait for her permission. Although the muscle strain was severe on his back, he got one hand under her knees, the other behind her back. He pushed himself out of the chair, stumbled across to the davenport, dropped her like she was a corpse instead of a healthy, beautiful woman.

She remained as he had dropped her. Her eyes were burning beacons and when he started to turn away, she held her arms up to him in a supplicating gesture.

'It's your husband,' he whispered hoarsely. 'I just heard him at the door.'

It wasn't fear that forced her erect. It was something that completely baffled Dan. Her fingers were completely unhurried and she reacted as if she didn't give a hoot in what compromising situation McGowan caught her.

Dan heard the door open and close, then a man's voice calling softly, 'Cleo! Are you up and decent?'

'In here, Clifton,' she answered easily. 'Dan's with me. We've been swimming. The water is delightful. Must be at least eighty five. Come in. I want you to meet him. He's been so kind to stay until you came home. Carl had another engagement that he swore he couldn't break. It was just like him. But I'm glad he did leave early. He can be such a bore at times.'

Dan dragged his glance away from the puzzling picture of his hostess, a tableau of trenchant nonchalance that was incredible. His eyes focused on a man, a tall, white-haired individual who stood eyeing him as if he was a prize bull and he was the appraiser.

'Mr. Daniel Slick, I believe,'

His voice was somewhat higher than Dan had looked for and its treble tones startled him. And the way McGowan studied him made his irritation rise. Why in hell did the man have to arrive home at the crucial moment of conquest? He asked himself bitterly. Why couldn't he have stayed away another ten or fifteen minutes at least?

Dan got hold of himself and climbed to his feet, suddenly feeling deeply chagrined and embarrassed at his costume or lack of it. There was nothing on beneath the big towel. He had dropped the trunks in the bath house. Cleo had left her suit lying on the flagstones. For the first time Dan realised what a compromising position he was in.

He had a momentary vision of his new managership flying out the window, then McGowan's high voice cut through the dreamy haze and brought him back to realities.

'It was very kind of you, Dan—I hope you don't mind my using your given name—to remain and entertain my wife until

I returned. I do hope you two can have many more evenings together. She needs the companionship of a younger man.'

Bewildered by McGowan's statements and even more puzzled by his wife's reactions to his arrival, Dan could do no more than mumble that he was delighted to meet Mr. McGowan.

Cleo had the gall to laugh at his discomfiture. 'He's a very shy man, Clifton dear. I do believe he was fearful that you might be angry with him because he had stayed so late.

McGowan glanced at his wrist watch and for the first time Dan got a good look at his eyes. They were like a pair of olives floating around in a bowl of milk. They were green and the irises seemed flecked with red. There was neither any expression in the eyes nor on the long angular face.

Dan felt like shaking his head and closing his eyes, then opening them again to see if what he was looking at was real. He had never heard of any man so willing to turn over his wife to a younger man It didn't make sense to him. There had to be a reason and for the first time he felt a small chill of apprehension.

Cleo and her husband appeared to have a most definite understanding of each other's behaviour There seemed to be a collusion as if each was working toward the same goal. Dan had a hunch that when he found out what that goal was he wouldn't like it Now that he thought back the entire evening seemed to have been planned and rehearsed The noise that Cleo had heard while they were in the pool could have been McGowan's first arrival, this one his second.

Perhaps, Dan thought with a tingling sensation, McGowan had witnessed the love scene. If he had, and still refused to comment or show anger, then there was something decidedly wrong with the scene.

CHAPTER NINE

DAN waited no longer to do what he thought was especially necessary under the circumstances. He felt like a fool talking to the head of the corporation he worked for, dressed in nothing but a huge bath towel. His clothes were out in the bath house, he excused himself, and hurried as fast as he could across the patio.

He dressed quickly and returned to the living room noting instantly that Cleo had also substituted the towel for dressing gown. Her husband sat in the big armchair with a huge cigar in his mouth, and they had quite obviously been discussing Dan for the conversation stopped abruptly as he entered.

McGowan motioned Dan to a chair as he said, 'I've been intending to pay you a visit, Dan, at your office. But with the press of this merger which I am trying to put together and my other many duties, I haven't had an opportunity. As this is more or less our home territory I decided to make a personal inspection of your office first. Briefly, I should like a resume of what you are doing, what you operate, and any other pertinent facts that might be useful in the betterment of the management.'

'How soon do you want it?' Dan was already up to his ears in weekly and monthly reports, in statistics of sales, in compiling a new selling manual for his sales force. But here was the head man. He was up there high enough to ask for and get what he wanted.

'One week from tonight,' McGowan told him.

He looked at Dan as if he expected either an argument or a protest.

'Will you call for it or do you wish it mailed?' Dan asked.

'Do you mean to tell me you can make out such a report in such a short time?' McGowan's eyebrows crescented quizzically.

'Most assuredly. That's the way I run my office, Mr. McGowan. Every day I know exactly how many cleaners have been sold, how many commissions were paid out, who sold them and where. I can tell you from memory how many new machines and duds are in the warehouse. I can give you the names and the quantity of parts that are on order, not from memory, but from my daily records. I know the full name of every salesman and with a small amount of mental calculation I can tell you what he earns per week, not exactly, but within a few pennies.'

'If you can do that,' McGowan told him, 'you're an exceptional young man and you're being wasted in the branch office. How much training have you had in the field?'

'A little more than six months. I can sell a Keen Kleaner to a cow if she can understand my lingo and has the money for a down payment. I know our cleaner. It's top merchandise and I don't think any other vacuum cleaner comes close to it.'

'Have you ever run into a cow that could understand your lingo?'

For the first time Dan caught a tiny twinkle of amusement in the cold eyes. Before Dan could reply, Cleo chimed in with, 'I sincerely hope you're not referring to me as a cow, Dan'

McGowan chuckled and Dan colored. 'Hardly', Dan assured her. 'As for running into a cow who can understand English, I'm afraid if I did, I'd take it on the run, certain that some one had either spiked my drink or I'd had too much.'

'Do you drink in excess, Dan?' McGowan asked.

'I'm not an alcoholic,' Dan told him with a small shrug. 'I suppose like everyone else who drinks, I occasionally imbibe too freely. When I do, I pay for my stupidity with a hangover, a really glorious one.'

'You're not married or engaged-'

Dan was wondering what all this questioning was leading up to, but he hoped it was advancement of some kind. If the old buzzzard wanted his life history, Dan was willing to give it to him.

'No marital ties or otherwise, Sir.'

'Excellent.'

McGowan climbed to his feet, snubbed his cigar out in an ash tray and stepped over to where his wife was curled up on the davenport. He leaned over and kissed her on the cheek straightened and looked at Dan.

'My office is in the Sunset Building. Never mind about the report tomorrow, but be in my office at nine sharp. Good night, Dan.'

He did not offer to shake hands. He left the room and a moment later Dan heard a door close.

Cleo said drily, 'You're in, Mister Man, Clifton likes you. I thought he would. But don't be late for that appointment. He loves punctuality.'

'In that case I'd better be on my way before I wear out my welcome,' Dan told her as he stood up.

She uncurled from the davenport, followed him to the front door, making no objections to his departure. He wondered if he ought to kiss her good night, but decided against it when she made no advances or gave any hints that such a caress was in order.

Once again he was ill-at-ease, almost shy. He mumbled a good night and his thanks for the meal and left.

Promptly at nine he was waiting in the outer office for his appointment with McGowan. His night's sleep had been restless and full of nightmares.

McGowan's secretary walked in and Dan caught his breath. Her hair was brushed back severely and fashioned into a figure eight at the nape of her neck. It was the color of milk chocolate and in spite of the plainness of the hair-do, it reflected the light like a polished mahogany desk. There were wide-spaced, deep blue eyes behind the horn-rimmed, gold-filigreed glasses, and a slightly upturned nose and a big mobile mouth above a small chin with a dimple that appeared and vanished with each word.

Dan decided that McGowan was no slouch when it came to picking his office help. This one was a real lovely in spite of the Puritanical costume and the phoney primness. He'd have been willing to bet that when the day's work was done, she could be excellent company.

'Mr. McGowan will see you now, Mr. Slick,' she announced with the ghost of a smile.

McGowan was behind his desk and he looked at Dan as if he had eaten something that didn't agree with him. He was the great stone face, Dan decided. He felt almost as ill-at-ease as he had the previous night when he had first arrived at the McGowan home. He wondered why he had been ordered to the head office and he was hopeful that it was something good. The big boss seemed to have liked him.

'I'll not beat around the bush, Dan,' McGowan said. 'You've seen my wife on several occasions, including the one last night. I think you'll agree that she is not only a lovely looking woman, but a most affectionate one.' Dan could feel the color rising up his throat and it irritated him. McGowan's only reaction was a faintly amused quirk around his thin lips.

'I believe, from the little I have seen of you,' McGowan continued easily, 'that you are the type of man who could not be closely associated with such a woman without becoming interested. And almost any male seems to have the same similar effects on my wife. I witnessed part of the romancing yesterday evening, Dan.'

Dan opened his mouth to murmur an apology. If the old man had seen all of that scene, he decided, then he was a gone gull as far as his job was concerned. An apology would hardly do any good at this late date. The best thing for him to do, was to keep his mouth close and let the chips fall where they may.

As if he had read Dan's mind, McGowan said, 'No apologies are necessary, Dan. Ten years ago, although I was considerably older than you are now, I met Cleo, I reacted the same way you did last night. Cleo's a most persistent young woman when she wants something. I may be wrong, but I think she wants you. Dan I'll lay my cards on the table. I want a divorce. I'll pay you ten thousand dollars cash if you will arrange it so that I can catch you in a compromising situation. You set it up. I'll have the photographer and the witnesses there to get the evidence.'

Dan felt like reaching across the desk and grabbing the old man by the throat and shaking him until his teeth rattled. The man was willing to pay money to another man to compromise his wife. It was about the lowest and vilest form of bribery Dan had ever heard of. And he felt sure that the first offer was not the last one. McGowan was a parsimonious, crusty old devil. Dan knew that if McGowan died while he was still married to Cleo, she would under the California laws, still get her widow's mite. McGowan didn't want her to to have even that much He was trying to make sure she got nothing.

There were two things that held Dan to his chair, that kept him from stalking out the office and telling the old man to go to hell. The first was Cleo. He felt sorry for her. She had given McGowan what he wanted and it was no fault of hers that he failed to appreciate it.

The second was the knowledge that McGowan was the big boss and the man who could do more for Dan than any other member of the organization. Dan didn't want to stop with just a branch managership. He wanted to be up top, up where McGowan and the other men were. And he was willing to sacrifice some principles in order to get there.

If he played along with McGowan, he might move much faster up the ladder. He might in fact hurdle all the lower echelons in one jump. An idea began to form somewhere in the back of his head, nebulous first then beginning to jell as the facts came together like the parts of a puzzle. Yet he knew that he had to play his hand close to his belly. McGowan hadn't reached his present exalted position without brains and hard work.

'I'm a cleaner salesman, Mr. McGowan,' he said. 'I started out punching doorbells, walking my legs off, beating my brains out trying to sell our product. I did a good job. It was good enough to get me promoted without your help or anyone else's. I'm damned ambitious. The spot where you're sitting is my goal. You can't live forever anymore than I can.'

'Then you don't like my offer.'

McGowan's eyes were like flaked ice. His lower lip folded under and he gripped it with his teeth. Dan could see the man was not only disappointed, he was angry to think that his judgment of a man had been bad.

'I didn't say that,' Dan answered, poker-faced and trying to hide his real feelings.

'Then don't beat around the bush,' McGowan snapped in his high voice.

'As far as making love to your wife is concerned,' Dan continued with a faint smile, 'I can't imagine any task that could be more agreeable. I've never seen another woman as pretty or with a more affectionate nature.' He saw the anger that began to mottle McGowan's face and he added quickly, 'I didn't mean that literally. But I don't have to tell you that. You've lived with her for ten years. I'm sure you know her much better than I do. It was my impression that she was not only lovely to look at. I gathered that her temperament matched her beauty. I think if she truly loved a man there is nothing she wouldn't do to prove that love.'

For the first time since they had met, Dan heard Clifton McGowan laugh. It lifted the corners of his lips in a grotesque grin that made Dan feel as if he needed a fur-lined overcoat. It had that same treble quality as his voice. The only thing Dan could imagine that could laugh like it would be a ghoul.

'You're not very observing or else you've had little experience with women like Cleo. After that interlude in the pool, you were quick to draw conclusions. Cleo is not by nature a warm-hearted person. To one who has known her as long as I have she's as transparent as a sheet of plate glass. Cleo lives for herself alone. No one else counts. You were no more than a means to an end. She loves clothes, jewels, the essential things of life as such or more than she loves any man. She will always be that way.'

Suddenly curious Dan asked, 'What does she see in Carl Mabee?'

'I should say that Carl interests her in a way of which I am not informed. He is a confirmed bachelor and a celibate. He lives with his widowed mother. He would never leave her for any woman, no matter how lovely she might be.'

'Did you make him an offer like you did me?' Dan asked.

McGowan shook his head. 'Hardly. Carl is not the type. Besides he is my attorney and he is very fond of both Cleo and myself. Well?'

The idea that had formed in the back of Dan's head was no longer nebulous. Making love to a woman of Cleo's temperament would be more than just an experience. Perhaps, he thought, if he went through with the deal he might end up with Cleo as his wife and Clifton McGowan as his office boy. The thing to do was to haggle, squeeze every drop he could out of the old buzzard and get some sort of a contract to protect himself.

'Ten thousand isn't enough,' Dan told him. 'You've got to realize my position. Entertaining your wife is going to cost me a pretty penny and it's a full time job. I can hardly remain as branch manager while I'm working at it. And once you have the evidence and the pictures I'll be a dead duck. Your wife will look on me as a pariah. Once the word gets out, the newspapers will crucify me. It should be worth a helluva lot more than ten grand. That is if you really want a divorce.'

'Name your price, Dan.'

Dan decided to shoot for the moon. It was glaringly apparent McGowan had been searching without success for a presentable man who would not only do his dirty work for him, but would keep his mouth shut. McGowan had reached the conclusion Dan Slick was that man. Cleo had fallen for his rugged looks. And he was a good salesman, which to McGowan was most essential.

'For a hundred thousand in cash and your signed agreement to make me a vice-president of Kleen Kleaners. I'll do what you ask. I'll not only do it,' Dan added, 'I'll guarantee the pictures and the evidence.'

'You drive a hard bargain, Dan,' McGowan protested. 'That's a lot of money. More money than most men manage to accumulate in a lifetime. How about fifty and no guarantee of a job afterwards?'

Dan laughed in his face, He felt sure he had McGowan over a barrel and he despised him enough to want to see him squirm.

'You heard my terms. You can take it or leave it.' Dan pushed his chair back and stood up, looking down into McGowan's long face and thinking how repulsive it was.

'You forget that your reputation will follow you,' McGowan hinted. 'What good will a vice-presidency be then.'

What McGowan said made a lot of sense, Dan thought quickly. He hadn't considered it from that angle. What he would have to have was something additional in the way of cash to make up for the job he'd lose.

'You asked for it, Mr. McGowan.' Dan placed his two hands on the desk and glared at his boss. 'A job with Keen Kleaners wouldn't be worth anything once I've fulfilled the contract. So we up the ante to a grand and a half. And believe me, I'll earn every dime of it before I'm finished.'

'I should hardly consider making love to my wife either an unpleasant or a difficult task,' McGowan sneered. 'All right. One hundred thousand.'

'Payable how?' Dan demanded. 'I've got to have new clothes, a new car, the works. And frankly, I'm no Lothario as you seem to think. I'm just a rough and tough Texan. I'll have to do some learning. This longhorn will have to be polished some before he can reach first base with your wife.'

'How soon can you start?'

Dan had expected more arguments, more haggling over the price. McGowan's acceptance caught him flat-footed. The more he thought about it, the more terrifying the idea became. McGowan might well have some ulterior motive in mind. Once Dan had set the stage and was ready to be photographed with

Cleo, what was to prevent Clifton McGowan from killing them both? Dan doubted if any jury in the state would convict him under such circumstances. He would tell the court and the world that he was simply defending his home against an unscrupulous thief who was trying to steal the one thing that McGowan held dearer than life itself.

Dan knew exactly where he'd end up. Buried in Potter's field, while the lovely Cleo got a gorgeous funeral with all the trimmings, and McGowan a hero's hurrahs.

CHAPTER TEN

I T WAS the tempting vista of a hundred thousand dollars in cash that made Dan force his fears into the background. There were ways to prevent McGowan from either killing him or having him killed. He could rent a safety deposit box and place a letter inside of it that would reveal the whole sordid contract if he was murdered.

'I can start tomorrow,' Dan said. 'All I have to do is cook up some tale about a special assignment from you and turn the office over to Norton. I'm sure he'll be delighted. But what about the pay and a contract?'

'Come back here at eleven then. I'll have ten thousand in cash and a contract for the balance.'

'On a hundred thousand dollar deal that isn't enough down payment,' Dan argued. 'Make it twenty five or it's no soap.' He was sure McGowan was so anxious to obtain evidence against his wife that he would pay without further quibbling.

'Twenty five thousand then,' McGowan agreed. 'The balance when you deliver.' He reached into the inside pocket of his coat and pulled out a leather wallet. He extracted ten one hundred dollar bills and passed them across the desk to Dan. 'There's a small bonus. Take the rest of the day off. Get yourself some clothes and find yourself a room in some respectable hotel. You don't have to change your name, but you do have to change your mode of living. Have some new cards printed. Call yourself, "Assistant to the Chairman of the Board, Keen Kleaners. Inc.". Give this address.

From now on you're working for me exclusively. It will give you a good credit rating. Get you past doors more easily If anyone makes inquiries I'll instruct my secretary what to tell them.'

He stood up and extended his hand. Dan looked at it with a sneer and shook his head. 'I wouldn't shake hands with your kind of man, McGowan. This is strictly a business deal. It it wasn't for the money, I wouldn't touch it with a ten foot pole. We might as well get the record straight. It is my considered opinion that you're about the lowest form of human life.'

McGowan's face began to mottle with his anger, but he managed to control his voice. 'Just what do you call yourself, Slick?'

'The second lowest form of human life.', Dan answered. 'See you in the morning.'

He wasn't sure what he felt like as he rode the elevator to the ground floor. He was partially numb at the prospect of earning a hundred thousand in one lump sum so easily. Yet in the back of his mind was the thought that something was definitely wrong with McGowan's deal. He had thought the previous night that McGowan and his wife were in collusion. But for the life of him he couldn't analyze in what way. If McGowan got the divorce, Cleo would get almost nothing. Her only chance was to outlive the old buzzard.

It struck him with the impact of a thrown rock. Perhaps that was her angle. Once she got Dan infatuated enough with her, maybe she intended to ask him to get rid of Clifton McGowan.

But such an idea, he told himself, was silly. Cleo wasn't that type of female. She was undoubtedly on the hot side, but she certainly wasn't a murderess. All she wanted was affection. Dan intended to give her that in large doses, and the sooner the better. He wanted that hundred thousand so bad he could taste it. Once he had it, he could take his pick of females. If he was tired of Cleo, he'd find some one else, Maybe Eddie.

He climbed into his old convertible and headed for his office. Eddie raised her eyebrows quizzically as he walked in nearly an hour late. Somewhat tartly she told him that Norton had conducted the sales meeting in his absence. Knowing that he had been a guest at the McGowan home she was filled with curiosity, but too full of pride to show it.

Dan satisfied it after he'd entered his office and checked his mail. He called her over the intercom. When she came in, he told her to sit down, offered her a smoke. When he told her about his new job as assistant Chairman of the Board, she looked as if some one had cut the ground from under her feet.

'Then Norton will take over as manager.'

Her dark eyes narrowed as she stared at Dan's face, seeing the color rise in it, and wondering. He didn't look like a man who has just been offered and accepted a job that paid a much larger salary. He seemed a total stranger, some one who wasn't too happy over his prospects, bright as he had painted them.

'And just what does the assistant to the big boss do for his wages?' she asked tartly. 'Entertain the lovely wife of the big boss? Is that why he hired you, Dan?'

He knew the color was rising up his throat and he somehow managed a fatuous laugh. 'Don't be silly, Eddie.' he protested. 'Nothing like that. McGowan wants some one he can trust to do investigative work for him. He's in the process right now of putting together a big merger. It will be my job to dig out facts for him, to find out about the officers of the other corporations. I'm supposed to dig up information that will be helpful to him,'

'But you will be seeing his wife', she persisted.

'Occasionally I suppose. There will be times when I'll undoubtedly have to report at his house.' He smiled at her. 'Aren't you interested in what happened last night, honey?'

'From the looks of you and the expression on your face,' she bridled, 'I've no doubt a good time was had by all. Norton gave me a little inside on the McGowan female.'

'That's ridiculous,' Dan parried. 'There was a Carl Mabee there for dinner too. He's McGowan's lawyer. Cleo didn't drink too much last night.'

'So now it's Cleo. My, but you're a fast worker!' Her eyes flashed.

'All her friends call her that.' he protested.

Eddie stood up, hands clenched at her sides, jealousy and anger giving her dark eyes a smoky cast. 'All her friends', she sneered. 'You can have her, Mr. Daniel Slick.'

Suddenly tears silvered her long lashes and a small sob caught in her throat. Dan jumped from the chair and caught her in his arms before she could protest. He held her with her face against his chest.

'There never has been anyone but you, Eddie.' he whispered. 'You should be congratulating me instead of getting angry. This is a step up the ladder. I'll be making twice as much as I am here, Frankly, it's not going to be easy. McGowan's a crusty old, parsimonious swine and I'll bet he's got the first dime he ever made. But he is the big boss and he can oil the wheels of my progress. Dry your eyes now and give me a nice big kiss.'

Damp-eyed she turned her head to stare up at his face. 'I thought it was against the rules for employers and employees to romance on company time.' She picked the handkerchief out of his pocket, wiped her eyes dry, returning the linen to its place in his costume. 'Not that I give a damn, you big lug. You must know by this time that I'm crazy about you.'

The kiss was long and satisfying and it made Dan feel more like a heel than ever. But he had to play the part, he told himself. Making love to Eddie and allaying her suspicions was part of it.

No one must ever know that he had been hired to gather divorce evidence.

'Dinner tonight, honey?' he asked. 'May be the last time for a little while. One of the firms in the merger is in the Frisco area. I might have to take the morning plane tomorrow. McGowan yells and old Danny Slick jumps.'

'Why not?' A smile lifted the corners of her lips and her eyes twinkled with some inner amusing and anticipatory thought. For a change I'll do my own cooking. I'm not bad if I do admit it. Wait till you taste my Beef Strogonoff.'

Dan was a perfectionist. He had to have everything in order before he turned the office over to Norton. He didn't take time out for lunch. He sent out for a sandwich and a cup of coffee. Promptly at five he was ready to leave. Norton had been informed, Dan's desk was cleaned out, and Eddie was waiting for him.

He drove her home, returned to his room to clean up and pack, told the landlady that he would be moving the next day. By six thirty he was ringing the doorbell at Eddie's place. She was still in the outfit she had worn to work. He kissed her and she broke away.

'Make yourself at home, darling.' she told him. 'I haven't had time to change. Now that you can watch the stove for me I'll slide out of this dress. Drag out some ice cubes and pour me a couple of fingers of bourbon neat. Help yourself to whatever you want.'

The bedroom door closed behind her. Dan had time to empty the ice tray, pour the bourbon, mix a Scotch over the rocks for himself and bring the mixings to the coffee table in front of the davenport. He could hear the shower running, the sound of auto horns, and even the pounding of his own heart.

He glanced around the apartment, remembering his thoughts the first time he had visited Eddie's home. He had decided then, that if she would go for it, he'd move in with her on a strictly platonic basis. When she had promptly turned down such an arrangement he had proposed marriage. He was glad now that she hadn't tied him up with an engagement. Eddie was one delightful and lovely person, but she wasn't for him. He had his sights set much higher now.

She reappeared in a whisper of satin, something bright red, an outfit that the advertisements called a negligee.

She had loosened her long hair, brushed it and left it to fall freely in soft waves to below her shoulders. It reflected the light as if it were polished ebony. Around her entire body was an aura of perfume. As she leaned over to pick up the shot glass of straight bourbon, the incredibly black hair made a waterfall about her face.

His hand shook as he lit two cigarettes and handed her one. She tossed the drink off with a single movement of her head, refilled the glass, then sat down beside him with her legs curled under her. She pushed the long black hair from her face with her hand and turned to smile at him.

Suddenly she sniffed the air and let out a small cry. 'Heavens! Something's burning.' She leaped from the davenport and scampered into the small kitchen.

She turned around and glanced at him. She caught the look in his eyes and on his face and she exclaimed gaily, 'How do I look, darling?'

'Like a million bucks,' he answered, his voice sounding hoarse in his ears. 'To hell with the Beef Strogonoff. Come back here and sit beside me.'

She shook her finger at him. 'Big strong men need food, darling. You had nothing but a sandwich for lunch and I'll bet you had very little breakfast if you were in McGowan's office at nine. You'll eat your Beef Strogonoff and like it. I want to convince you that your fiancée is an excellent cook as well as a pretty wench.'

Dan almost winced at the remark. He had asked her to marry him often enough and she refused. Now when he was no longer sure, she was willing to accept his proposal, had as a matter of fact announced that she was his fiancée.

'I'll eat it,' he groaned. 'But I don't like the idea. You're driving me to drink.'

'Why do you think I wore this outfit?' she asked coquettishly and pirouetted. 'Now that I've got competition from a blonde I have to use every wile to hold what I want.'

She gave the contents of the saucepan another fillip of stirring, then retuned to where he sat. His glass was nearly empty and without asking him, she refilled it to overflowing from the Scotch bottle, then poured another hooker of bourbon for herself.

He frowned at the old fashioned glass, looked at her and he asked, 'You trying to get me plastered in a hurry, honey? That was at least four fingers you dumped into my glass.'

'I'm way ahead of you, darling.' She downed the bourbon with a single toss of her head, spread out the negligee around her like a fan as she sat down. 'Drink yours. I've been tippling ever since I came home. That was my fifth bourbon. So far you've only had one over the rocks.'

He shrugged. 'If that's the way you want it, honey.' He picked up the glass, drained it and set it back on the table. An idea came to him, one that sounded amusing and he said, 'I don't believe you're what you said.'

Her eyebrows raised. 'You wouldn't have ulterior motives, Mr. Slick? Now would you?'

He forced his face into a sober pattern. 'You malign me, wench.'

The telephone when it rang sounded so loud it startled them both. Dan was closest to it. He let go of Eddie reluctantly and took the instrument off its cradle. When he answered, McGowan's high voice squeaked against his ear drum.

Dan listened with a face that grew longer and longer. When he placed the instrument back, he looked at Eddie and shook his head. 'The big boss,' he explained. 'Has to leave for Frisco tonight. Wants me in his office on the double. Sorry honey.'

'You should be,' she screamed back, her face twisting with rage.

CHAPTER ELEVEN

SHE was in no mood for apologies and Dan knew it. He wouldn't have blamed her if she had thrown an ash tray or something else equally handy as he opened the door. But she didn't. She followed a woman's prerogative and burst into tears. Frustrated and furious at McGowan for the selfishly inconsiderate interruption, Dan rode the elevator to the first floor, hurried out to the street and climbed into his convertible.

Much to his surprise McGowan's secretary was in the outer office. She had apparently just finished her work for her boss. She was patting make-up on her face with a compact and coloring her lips. The horn-rimmed glasses were gone and Dan was even more startled by the change in her looks. She seemed taller than he remembered and the dimple in her chin turned on and off like a flashing neon sign each time she moved her lips while applying the rouge.

'You can go right in, Mr. Slick,' she said with what he could only analyze as a sly look, as if she knew exactly what was going on between Dan and her boss.

Having just left the beginnings of a good dinner and the prospect of a wonderful evening, Dan was hungry and highly irritated at his luck. He knew that he'd have no chance of returning to Eddie's and taking up where he had left off. If he tried to get back in, he was sure she would either throw something heavy at trim or call the police.

He had tried to convince himself that it was better that way. He couldn't afford to become emotionally involved with Eddie, not while he was trying to get somewhere with Cleo McGowan Yet the prospect of spending an evening alone was so dismal, that the moment he looked at this chocolate-haired girl, the idea hit him hard.

'If you're not otherwise engaged,' he said. 'My business with your boss will only take a minute or two. I'm sadly in need of a dinner companion. Sorry, but I don't know your name.'

'Shelby,' she dimpled. 'Shelby Dorrance.' The smile she handed him was packed with authority. 'As a matter of fact I had no place to go but my apartment. But I'd better not wait for you here. Mr. McGowan might not approve. I'll meet you downstairs in the Pitcairn Bar. It's hard right of the main entrance and about half way down the block.'

McGowan's treble voice squealed through the glass partition. 'Is that you, Slick? Walk in. I'm in a hurry.'

'Sold,' Dan grinned at her. 'Give me about fifteen minutes.'

She nodded brightly and vanished into the corridor. Dan opened McGowan's door and crossed the room to his employer's desk. He was so blinded by the sight of a package of bills that he scarcely looked at McGowan.

'All right, Dan,' McGowan prodded. 'It's the money we agreed upon. You don't have to look so damned greedy. Haven't you ever seen that much money before?'

Dan chuckled. 'Not outside of a bank and never close enough to touch. Come on, Let's get this over with. I'm anxious to get to work. There's another seventy five grand coming when the job is done. Don't forget that. And I might add that this trip to your office was damned inconsiderate and inconvenient.'

McGowan smiled icily. 'I guessed as much when I finally found you in Miss Goes apartment. A most attractive brunette, Dan. Your current light-o'-love, I believe.'

Dan's eyes turned as icy as McGowan's and he slammed his fist down on the desk. 'You keep your insults to yourself, Mister,' he snarled. 'Eddie's a good friend and nothing more. Quit beating around the bush. Show me the contract.'

McGowan pushed a single sheet of bond paper across the desk. 'Read it and see if it meets your terms. And no offense intended regarding Miss Goes. I don't disapprove. The knowledge that you were one of the few men in the office whom she regarded highly had some weight in my choice of you for my wife.'

Dan neither liked the word he had used nor the manner in which he said it. 'You'll keep a civil tongue in your head, McGowan, or I'll twist that skinny neck of yours. The more I see of you, the less I like your looks.'

'But you like the color of this.' McGowan patted the bundle of bills and smiled blandly.

Dan got a grip on his temper and yanked the chair up close to the desk. He read the contract through twice. Everything they had agreed upon seemed there. He was no lawyer, but he couldn't find any holes that McGowan might crawl out of. The chocolate-haired Shelby Dorrance was waiting for him at the Pitcairn Bar. Another lovely, Cleo McGowan, would be expecting him not later than the next evening or maybe earlier. And Dan was anxious to get his hands on that bundle of money, feel it, count it, and think of all the things he could do with it.

But the conscience he thought was buried deep was suddenly back to plague him. He'd already given up his manager's job to Norton. If he wanted to, he couldn't go back. McGowan, he was sure, wouldn't permit it. That evening had finished him with Eddie. He'd walked out on her at the wrong time. And once she found out what he was doing and intended to do, she'd treat him like an outcast.

Dan wasn't worried so much about the tabloids. He doubted if McGowan would like too much publicity and he was sure the tycoon wouldn't want the world to know that he'd been betrayed. If Dan turned down the contract at this late date, he was finished in the area. He had no doubts on that score.

Dan took the pen that McGowan offered, signed the contract and received the bundle of money. He started to remove the paper band and count it and McGowan told him to save that for a later date, that he had to catch a late plane. Then he stood up to signify that the conference was over.

'Where's my copy with your signature?' Dan demanded suspiciously.

McGowan's smile was thin. 'You get no copy, Dan. This one goes into my safety deposit box.'

Dan jumped from his chair and tried to grab the agreement. McGowan pulled back, snatched a revolver from his desk drawer, waved Dan back.

'There is no need to jump to conclusions,' McGowan counseled. 'There is no need to get panicky. My word is as good as my bond. You should understand that a contract such as this would be looked upon by the courts as a conspiracy. You might even use it to blackmail me afterwards.'

Dan didn't like the idea, yet he knew that what McGowan said had the ring of truth. Besides the agreement was signed and if Dan tried to take it away from McGowan he would end up with a bullet through his guts. He felt sure that McGowan wouldn't aim for any other spot. The man had a streak of cruelty running through him.

Dan pocketed the bundle of money, stood up and glared at McGowan. 'Just one more thing for the record, you parsimonious old skunk! For some reason it was a relief to tell McGowan exactly what he thought of him. 'In case you have any ideas of having me bumped off after I've done your dirty work, just remember this. I'll have a safety deposit box of my own and in it I'll give all the details. They may not hang my murder on you, but they'll sure as hell make life miserable for a while.'

'I have no intention of having you killed,' McGowan answered with furious eyes. 'And you can save your names for your guttersnipe friends. Now get out of here.'

Stalking through the outer office, Dan got a sudden idea. He didn't trust McGowan nor did he like the idea of carrying so much money in a single bundle. He noticed the wardrobe closet in the corner and on impulse he opened the outer door, slammed it shut and quickly fitted his big frame into the closet.

He had no more than closed the door when he heard McGowan talking to some one on the phone. It was a short conversation and Dan couldn't distinguish any of it. A moment later McGowan crossed the outer office, the door closed and when Dan peeked out, the room was dark and he heard the elevator as it rose to pick up its client.

When he heard the elevator descending, Dan pussy-footed out into the darkness, switched on the lights and opened the typewriter desk that Shelby Dorrance used. He found a box of 18 pound bond and a pair of scissors. He cut a stack of the paper into the approximate size of the money bundle, removed the bank's band, and made up a new bundle with a hundred dollar bill on the top, some of his own smaller ones beneath, and another hundred on the bottom. The real money he distributed about his person, some under his shirt, some inside his sox, some in the other pockets.

If McGowan had hired a man or men to waylay him and relieve him of that twenty-five grand, and if they found the thick bundle first, he hoped they'd forget about the rest of him and run for it.

Back on the street again, he looked to right and left, couldn't see anyone who seemed suspicious and walked down the street to the Pitcairn Bar. He found Shelby Dorrance tapping her fingers on the table top in exasperated annoyance at his tardiness. He made quick apologies as he sat down beside her in the booth.

'The old buzzard kept me longer than I expected; he told her.

They had a pair of Martinis and Dan asked her if the food at the Pitcairn was any good. She said it was fair, but not too hot, and suggested a place on the strip.

'Did you get your money' she asked with a touch of malice in her blue eyes.

He gave her a startled look. 'You mean you know about the deal?'

'Why not? Somebody had to type the agreement.'

'Then you have a carbon?'

Dan's heart began to pound faster. If Shelby Dorrance had a copy of the agreement, then his life was a lot safer than he had feared.

'Certainly I have a carbon. I make carbons by second nature. This one looks like it might be worth a bundle to some one.'

Dan's eyes narrowed. She was easy on the eyes and the trip from well-shod feet to the top of her chocolate rich hair was pleasant. What surprised him was that underneath that thick mop of hair was a good set of brains that she knew how to use.

'You surprise me no end,' he grinned. 'First time I got a look at you I thought you were on the prissy side, just another secretary who spent her days making chicken tracks and tickling an IBM. Tonight you could have knocked me over with a paper match stick. Brother! Did I size you up all wrong! You're not only luscious to look at, there's a nice slug of brains under the lovely head of hair. Tell me, gorgeous. Is that hair the natural color or is it a rinse? I don't believe I've ever seen a head of hair just like it.'

'More or less natural,' she dimpled. 'Just a rinse to bring out the high lights.'

'At first I thought it was like milk chocolate,' he told her. 'Now I'm not so sure. Under these lights it looks more like bitter-sweet.' He beckoned to the waitress, ordered another pair of very dry Martinis, double ones, and when Shelby offered a faint protest, he told her that after they had that round, they'd head for the strip.

The drinks arrived, Dan paid with a bill from his wallet that he carried in his hip pocket, and then for some reason which he couldn't at the moment analyze he patted his inside coat pocket.

'Long as you know about the deal, I'll give you a quick peek.'

He opened his coat and when she leaned forward to peer inside, he lifted the money bundle just far enough for her to read the hundred on the top bill. He closed his coat quickly and got his arm around her shoulders before she leaned back.

'Twenty-five grand, gorgeous,' he whispered. 'And seventy-five more when the deal's consummated.'

'It's an awful lot of money,' she remarked with a quick look at him. 'But doesn't it make you feel like a heel, Dan?'

'For that much dough I don't mind feeling like a heel. Besides have you ever seen Cleo McGowan?'

Her lids half closed as she looked at him. 'I've seen ber.' Her voice was soft, and bitter as acid. 'If I were a man, I'd love to do exactly what you're doing. She deserves everything she gets, believe me.'

Dan chuckled. 'Sounds like you don't like her.'

Shelby shrugged her slim shoulders. 'I scarcely ever bother to hate anyone. But Cleoney is something else again. She's made life miserable for Clifton. He's given her everything. A wonderful home, servants, all the money she can spend, and what does she give him?'

Dan frowned. 'I wondered about that. What does she give him?'

She glanced at him quickly and then away. 'She gives him exactly nothing but a bad time. He's the most ill-treated man I've ever known.'

'Sounds to me like you have,' he told her with a faint smile.

'What if I have?' she hedged.

He laughed.

She bridled. 'Whatever I did was out of sympathy. And Clifton appreciated it. Believe me.'

'But you'd cut his throat and sell that carbon of our agreement to the highest bidder.'

'I have to look after my own interests,' she bickered. 'I know you have no copy of it, and I know you'd like one. It would be good insurance. Like to make an offer, Dan, darling.'

She put her hand on his and squeezed it. 'You're my kind of man. I knew it the first time you walked into the office. We could go a long ways together. With a hundred thousand, think how far we could travel. Maybe I'm not as pretty as Cleo or that Miss Goes.'

'So you know Eddie Goes?'

Dan was beginning to think that the surprises would never cease. And he knew that Shelby Dorrance would be a good one to have on his side. She might make a valuable witness if one was ever needed. She seemed to know McGowan's office inside and out. She was apparently in his confidence.

Dan pulled Shelby tighter against his shoulder as he lifted his glass. 'You know something, honey. Eddie is a real pretty brunette, but if I was a beauty judge I'd line you up ahead of her. And if your boss told you that Eddie Goes was my girl, I can tell you it's a damned lie. Sure, I was practically engaged to her, but tonight the curtain went down for keeps. We bid each other a very frosty good-bye.'

She glanced at her wrist watch. 'I don't know about you, but I'm getting hungry, Dan darling. Romance is wonderful and I could listen to you all night when you say such lovely things, but all I had for lunch was a low calory salad and a cup of black coffee. Besides I never could drink Martinis. Either this plastic seat is steam heated or I am Let's go some place and dance. I have a feeling that I'd like to be in your arms, even if it is out in public.'

The night was unusually balmy. Dan dropped the top down, fastened it in place, climbed in beside Shelby who immediately slid close to him and linked one hand under his arm.

After he had gunned the motor and moved out into traffic, she said, 'I've got a better idea. Let's stop at a drive-in for a hamburger, then go on out to Mulholland Drive and park. It's too nice a night to be inside. And I can still feel your arms around me.'

'Sold to the highest bidder,' Dan agreed.

The hamburgers were tasty, the coffee black and steaming and while they ate, Dan learned a little of Shelby's background and he told her of his. At her suggestion he stopped at a liquor store and bought a pint of bourbon.

They found a nice dark spot on the drive that gave them a view of the city and that was fairly secluded from other parkers. Dan cut the motor. With no urging Shelby turned on the seat with her back to Dan and her feet up over the door. She eased back until his arm supported her. She lifted one arm and locked it around his neck. She looked up at his face in the faint gleam of the dash lights.

'This is what I wanted all the time, Dan darling.'

Her voice was a whisper of sound. He heard nothing but the unintelligible words she muttered. Then something crashed against his skull, dropping him into instant oblivion.

CHAPTER TWELVE

DAN had never felt so utterly bone-weary in his life. He couldn't seem to open his eyes, or move any of his muscles. Then dimly as if from a great distance he heard a man's voice saying, 'Seems to be coming around now, lady. Did you get a good look at the two men?'

A girl's voice answered. 'It was like I told you, officer. It's real dark and neither of us heard them. Dan was behind the wheel and I was—well, across his lap. He's my fiance. All I can tell you is that their faces were covered with some kind of a mask, sort of funny like. I could see them through them, but their features were all flattened out.'

'Sure,' the officer agreed. 'Silk stockings. Flattens out the nose and makes the features unrecognizable. Did your boy friend lose any large amount of money?'

'I don't know. I saw them take something that looked like a bundle of money out of the inside pocket of his coat.'

Dan opened his eyes fully, focusing them on the group that stood above him. He was stretched out on the ground, with a coat under his head. There were two policemen and a girl The girl's hair was unpinned and fell like a dark waterfall to her shoulders. Her blouse was torn and she was holding it together with two fingers of her left hand. Her skirt was ripped.

Dan let out a groan and one of the officers leaned over him. 'How do you feel, Mister? Able to give us a statement now? Did you lose anything?'

Memory flooded back and Dan pushed his hand into the inside pocket of his coat. The big bundle of phony bills with the good ones on top were gone, but when he ran his hand over his shirt at the belt line he could feel the bulge of the real bills.

He sat up and with the officer's hand under his elbow, climbed rockily to his feet. He leaned against the side of the car, trying to reconstruct the evening's events, staring at the girl, at first not remembering who she was, then suddenly aware that it was McGowan's secretary. He wondered instantly if she was in cahoots with her employer to have Dan robbed. It was she who had suggested the Mulholland hide-away for a bit of necking. She knew of his deal and she knew that he was carrying a bundle of money.

He shook his head to clear it and the movement sent shafts of pain down his neck 'Afraid 'I can't help you much, officers,' he told them finally. 'Whatever it was they sapped me with, it did the work fast. I didn't know what hit me. I went out like a light. I guess your arrival must have scared them off. I had some insurance papers in my inside coat pocket that might have looked like bonds or money to them. Anyhow they're gone, but they aren't worth anything. I'll get copies of them tomorrow. Brother! My head feels like it had been through a meat grinder.'

He stared at Shelby and managed a weak smile. 'Looks like they worked you over a little too, honey. Hope you're all right.'

She came over and stood beside him, putting one arm around his waist. 'Thank God they didn't kill you, Dan darling. They frightened me out of my wits. They pulled me out of the car feet first, then grabbed you. You were unconscious. Are you sure you didn't lose anything important?' she added with a worried frown.

'Relax,' he told her. He looked at the two officers. 'Might as well chalk this one up to person or persons unknown. I imagine my head will have a bump the size of an egg on it in the morning, but I guess I can suffer through it. Thanks for the help. Come on, honey.' he added to Shelby. 'Let's get to hell out of here. I could use a drink and some cold packs on my noggin.'

Putting two and two together, Dan was beginning to think he had been played for a sucker by a very smart frail. In some ways it looked as if McGowan had set it up to deprive him of every red cent before he even became Cleo's paramour. And that, Dan thought, bitterly, was about as low a trick as a man could play yet not outside the limits of a stinker like Clifton McGowan who believed in giving no one a break.

Shelby's continued silence and anxious look did much to bring him to that belief. She had suggested that she had been out with McGowan and that he had appreciated it indeed. She seemed to feel that her boss had been taken when he had married Cleo. On the other hand how could she have known that Dan would invite her out to dinner?

They reached the strip and Dan suggested a drink at one of the bars. She countered with. 'I just don't feel up to it, Dan darling. Not the way I look. My blouse is in ribbons and my skirt's ripped all the way to my waist. It will take more than a couple of pins to hold it. My apartment is close by. I've plenty of ice and liquor.' She spoke doubtfully, as if she feared her invitation might be taken too literally.

The thought gave him a pleasant glow of anticipation. She had kissed like she'd enjoyed it. His memory hadn't failed him to that extent. On the other hand, if she had acted as the bait, then he felt sure that once the men who had sapped him found that all they had stolen was a few hundred bucks, they would follow and make another stab at getting the rest of the money.

Dan had an idea that he'd like very much to tangle with the two goons, but not without a weapon of some sort. He had no gun and had never carried one. But he did know how to shoot. The Navy had taught him that. And he also wanted to find out for sure if the luscious Shelby Dorrance was on the square.

Then he remembered the money he had stuffed behind various items of his clothing. He wondered what he could do with that, where he could hide it. He got the idea from a story he had read, how the holdup victim had stuffed her jewellery behind the seat. He remembered the other idea from what one of his customers had told him who'd been to Las Vegas. Fearing she might be held up on the way home and her winnings taken from her at the point of a gun, she'd tucked the bills into several envelopes and mailed them to herself.

'Sounds like an excellent idea,' he told Shelby. 'You got a gun in your apartment?'

'A gun? What on earth would I want with a gun? Heavens no. And why a gun? Are you expecting to shoot me?'

'If I had any proof that you lured me up to the skyline so some one else could rob me,' he assured her grimly, 'I wouldn't waste any time shooting you. I can think of better ways to retaliate.'

'But, Dan! I didn't. I swear it.' Her voice was nearly shrill in denial.

'Okay, honey. But you see what I mean. If I go to your apartment and those goons follow us, I'm going to be in trouble.'

'But they got your money. I saw one man lift that bundle of bills from your inside coat pocket.'

'You saw what looked like a bundle, honey. I'll explain after I get you home. Where do I turn?'

'Rossmore,' she directed. 'Then south to 5th. Right and there you are.'

Dan had no trouble finding the apartment and he hadn't seen any vehicle that looked as if it was following. He parked in front of the three storey building and while Shelby was climbing out and heading for the entrance, Dan managed to find the various bundles of money and to stuff them behind the seat. Shelby called to him in an impatient voice, demanding to know what was delaying him.

'Just a second, honey,' he answered. 'Something wrong with my light switch.'

To make it look right, he turned the switch off and on a couple of times while he watched the street behind through the rear view mirror. Although it was early, there was very little traffic on 5th and nothing that looked suspicious.

He followed Shelby through the plate glass door, up to the second floor and into her apartment. No longer bothering to hold her blouse or skirt together, she switched on the lights, told Dan to make himself to home while she changed.

'Fill up the ice bucket and use one of those dish towels for your head. I'll be out in a jiff.' She stood looking up at him with a worried frown. 'Honest to God, Dan. I had nothing to do with that robbery attempt. You do believe me, don't you?'

'Sure, honey.' He brought her in close and kissed her forehead first, then her full lips.

With a suppressed giggle, she broke away and vanished into her bedroom.

Dan went into the kitchenette, emptied two trays of ice cubes into the bucket, make a compress for his head and fired up a smoke. He was just beginning to take note of his surroundings when the drapes behind him parted and a man's voice told him to freeze.

'I kind of thought you'd be around,' Dan said with a great deal more nonchalance than he felt. 'Been waiting long?'

'Long enough to start sending down roots,' the man replied with a snarl. 'Quit stalling, Slick. You know what I'm after. That was a cute trick rigging up that bundle of paper to look like the real McCoy. Where's the real money? If I wasn't in a hurry I'd sap you again.'

'Sorry,' Dan told him with a shrug. 'If you wish, you can search me. If that wasn't the real stuff, then our mutual friend McGowan pulled a fast one.'

'You're crazy.'

Dan removed the icebag from his head and turned slowly. The man had stepped in front of the drapes and much to Dan's surprise he wasn't as big as his voice sounded. He was a wiry little squirt with a big head and a pair of ears that stuck out of his head like semaphores. The eyes above the crooked nose were small and closeset, and they were dark with anger.

'So I'm crazy. Like a fox. I don't know who you are, Mister, and I don't much care, but I do know you're a stupid little SOB and so is McGowan to think that I'd be silly enough to prowl the streets with twenty-five grand in cash.'

'Then where did you cache it?' the man demanded with a curse.

'With Uncle Sam.'

The little man looked nonplussed. 'Who the hell is Uncle Sam and where's his hangout? In the Sunset Building, I'll bet.' A snub-nosed revolver appeared in his left hand unexpectedly and almost mysteriously, making Dan wonder where the gun had been hidden.

Dan inhaled from his smoke and grinned. 'There's a small branch office there, my friend, although it is not the headquarters. For your information there's a mail shoot that leads from every floor to a box on the ground. And to enlighten you and satisfy your curiosity, I divided the bundle into ten piles, tucked each into an envelope, addressed it to my bank, stamped it, and dropped all ten down the shoot. If you want the twenty-five grand bad enough, I'm afraid you'll have to tamper with the

United States mails. Nor am I certain it is still there. I believe there was a pick-up about an hour ago.'

'Why you—' The little man took a step toward Dan and lifted the gun. 'You're too Goddamned smart for your own good. I think just for the helluva it I'll put a slug in your guts.'

'You and who else?' Dan asked with deceptive softness and moved fast.

He got one hand on the muzzle of the gun, the other around the little man's waist. He brought the wrist up and over his shoulder, threw his hip into the little man's midriff and with a single heave, sent him over his head and flying spread-eagled across the room. Dan was on him in a second after he hit the wall. He gripped him by the neck, brought his balled right fist up from the floor and slugged the little man back and forth until the man was a whimpering, drooling and pleading beggar.

Shelby heard the commotion and came out the bedroom. 'For God's sake, Dan. Stop it. You'll kill him and you'll have the police here.'

Dan laughed grimly. 'I was merely repaying this little squirt for the sapping job he did. Now I intend to find out who hired him.'

'Why ask him?' Shelby demanded impatiently. 'Isn't it plain enough? Clifton had no intentions of letting you keep that money. Nor do we intend to let you.'

Dan had been so intent on the little man that he had failed to see the automatic in her right hand. His first reaction was surprise, the second sorrow at the knowledge that she had been the bait, the third one a growing anger that he had been taken in.

'I guess you didn't hear what I told your pal here,' he shrugged. 'Uncle Sam's got the money in his custody and will keep it till the bank opens in the morning. So put the gun away, gorgeous. I think I've had my bellyful of both you and your friend.'

'I'll shoot,' she threatened.

'You haven't got the guts, you female Benedict Arnold. Sometimes I wonder why the good Lord puts such nefarious characters into such attractive bodies. Clifton isn't going to like this a little bit when you make your report. As the Mexicans say, "Hasta Manana".'

He wasn't too sure if she did have the guts, but he was counting on his judgment. There had been a ring of truth in her statement that he was her kind of man. But he breathed a lot easier when he reached the street and his convertible.

He was even more relieved when no vehicles followed him and he reached his room with the money intact and back inside his clothes.

He was up bright and early, breakfasted in his cafe, and packed his clothes. He paid off his landlady, and headed for the Cad agency that he had passed the previous day. He got a good trade on his old jalopy and came out driving a new convertible with wire wheels and everything on it but the kitchen stove. He was still laughing at the way the salesman had gawked when Dan paid cash from his heavy bank roll.

'You must be from Texas,' the man simpered.

Dan hit him a playful pat on the back that almost knocked him over. 'Sho enough am, Mister. The great sovereign state of Texas. Usually buy me these by the dozens, but I ran a little short and had to add one real fast to my stable. See you in church.'

Later he bought two new suits, a cashmere sport coat, three extra pair of slacks and the accessories to go with them. He told the salesman he was new in town and would call and tell him where to have the clothes delivered.

The Devonshire off Wilshire was a small respectable hotel. He got a room with bath, paid a week in advance then called the men's furnishing store and told them where he was. Around the corner was a branch of the Bank of America. He opened a checking account with five thousand as a starter, bought a small safety deposit box and put the rest of the cash in that. The young woman in charge of the vault brought him a sheet of paper and an envelope. He wrote the deal with McGowan plain enough for anyone to read if the box was opened after his death, tucked it in with the money, received his key and returned to the street.

He had lunch in a small bar and cafe on Wilshire, returned to his room, called Cleo and made a date with her for the evening. She sounded overjoyed to hear from him. She told him that she had called his office, but that the young woman had told her that he no longer worked there.

'I was terribly upset, darling,' she cooed.

'Your husband gave me a new job,' he informed her. 'Tell you all about it tonight. Until then, angel.'

'Love me?' she asked.

'More than I ever loved anyone.'

He knew what he intended to do when he hung up. If McGowan hadn't kept the original agreement and refused Dan a copy, if he hadn't laid a trap and tried to take the money away from him, Dan would have made good his end of the bargain. Now he didn't intend to unless he had more proof that McGowan would pay the balance. He was almost positive that McGowan had never intended to go through with his end. He wanted the divorce evidence bad enough and he was willing to pay something for it, but not a hundred thousand in cold cash.

Dan dressed carefully. He put on the new navy blue flannel suit, a white shirt, a conservative tie and black shoes. He wanted to show Cleo that he wasn't just another big lug. But after he had looked at himself in the mirror he came to the painful conclusion that clothes did not make the man. His features were too rugged and bony. He was still just another big lug.

Cleo looked even more lovely than she had the last time he'd seen her and now the tables were reversed. He had at first felt sorry for her husband, sorry because he was tied to a woman who cared only about herself. Now it was Cleo who had earned his entire sympathy. McGowan was a stinker of the first water and he was using underhanded methods to obtain a divorce, and dis-inherit his wife.

Finished with dinner and while they sat on the big chaise longue sipping brandies and coffee, Dan told her of his agreement with McGowan and of how much he was being paid.

Her long lashes veiled her topaz eyes, but he could almost feel her reaction, silent though it was until she asked softly, 'But why tell me, Dan darling?'

'For the simple reason that I intend to do everything I can to double-cross the old SOB.'

She turned her body a little to face him. 'That's simple enough if you have the guts, Dan.'

'You tell me, my sweet,' he promised, 'and I'll do my best.'

'If he should die,' she suggested with a faint smile. 'All of his money would revert to me as his only heir. It's as simple as that. Are you a good shot, Dan darling?'

CHAPTER THIRTEEN

SHE was all a man would want, wrapped up in a tight-fitted printed silk dress. From the top of her curly platinum head to the soles of her plastic heeled shoes, she was like a Caribbean cruise in the season, nothing but sunshine. The topaz eyes watched him with a look that seemed part amusement at his shocked reaction to her suggestion and part fear that he might not respond to her desires.

Dan's hand trembled a little as he picked up the brandy snifter glass and sipped at the liquor. What she had hinted had never entered his head. And the fact that she had made the suggestion, seemed even more out of character.

The dress had a background of chartreuse with gray and scarlet flamingos marching up and down the beautifully draped fabric. It seemed to swirl up her slim body.

As he remained silent she asked, 'Have I so shocked you that you can't even open your mouth, Dan?'

Dan shook his head. 'I was just thinking. I guess you know what they do to murderers in this state. They shove them into a little house with a plate glass window. They lock them in a chair so they can't move. Then they start dropping cyanide pellets into a pail of acid. The gas strangles the murderer. They say it's a more or less painless way to die, very humane, and simpler than hanging. Frankly, the thought of dying in that manner doesn't appeal to me. There's an old saying, you can do it better with gas, but I'm damned if I believe it.'

'Did you say they used cyanide pellets?' she asked with faintly excited curiosity. 'Isn't that the same stuff the gardener uses to kill gophers? I seem to remember seeing a can in the garage.'

'That's cyanogas,' Dan explained 'Similar, but not as potent as what they use up at the death house. If it was as concentrated you couldn't buy it so easily. Oh, I suppose you could die from breathing too much of it, especially if you had heart trouble.'

She lifted her glass and sipped, then turned to look at him. 'It's my opinion that most murderers are stupid. They always leave something behind, some clue that ties them in with the killing. There must be such a thing as a perfect crime. After all we are both intelligent people and there are hundreds of unsolved murders which goes to prove my point that you can get away with murder if you try hard enough.'

She placed her glass back on the side table, moved her feet off the chaise, then dropped the upper part of her torso back until her shoulders were against and supported by Dan's arm, the way she had done it before. He brought her head up with his hand and his mouth closed on hers. It seemed even better than the last time and he tried to set his glass on the table, but succeeded in doing exactly the same thing, dropping the snifter to the flag-stone terrace.

'That's two snifters I owe you,' he said as the glass tinkled.

She ran her hand along the ridge of his jaw in a soft caress. 'I'm mad about you,' she breathed. 'Simply mad about you.'

'Trying to soften me up?' he asked.

She giggled. 'You don't need any softening up, my darling. If I wanted to, I could wrap you around my little finger like a piece of string.' She dropped her head to his shoulder and she added, 'I've been thinking how wonderful it would be married to you. Just think of all the things we could do. Especially if we had Clifton's money. The first place I'd go would be to South America. Calypso music, rumbas, sambas, mambos, and those wonderful fiestas. Clifton won't go any place. He despises travelling. Except on business. Do you know something? I've been married ten years and I've never been out of this state.'

'Not even to Tijuana or Vegas?'

'Neither spot. Clifton hates the Mexicans and Las Vegas. He says it's not a place for a respectable young married woman.'

The latter I'll agree with, but not the former. There's no warmer race than the Mexicans and their kindness and hospitality exceeds all bounds. I was stationed at San Diego for a while in the Navy. Across the border was one of our favourite spots. Believe me. They treated us royally.

'Then there's Hawaii,' she said. 'They say it's beautiful. Can't you imagine the two of us on the beach at Waikiki? Riding the surf boards or the outriggers.' She sighed and snuggled a little closer.

'Sounds wonderful, my angel, but what would we use for money? Sure I've got most of the twenty-five grand your husband handed me and tried to take back, but—'

She sat up and stared at him. 'What do you mean he tried to take it back?'

He told her how he'd been played for a sucker by Shelby Dorrance, how she had finally admitted that she had been the bait.

Cleo's eyes narrowed in quick jealousy. 'Did you kiss her? Is that how they managed to sneak up on you?'

'Unless my memory plays me false,' he lied, 'it was the other way around. She got a strangle hold on me and they sneaked up from behind. When I came to, the cops were there and the phoney package of bills was gone.'

'But you went to her apartment,' she prodded irritably.

'Had to take her home and besides I wanted to find out if she was in cahoots with your husband.'

'Did you kiss her good night?'

'My sweet, you don't kiss girls good night when they have a gun pointed at your belly and they're threatening to shoot you if you leave. Believe me. By that time I was in no mood to kiss Shelby Dorrance.'

'Do you think she's as pretty as I am?'

He grinned at her and pulled her back against his chest. 'Neither as pretty nor as smart. And when she as much as admitted as having gone with your husband, I crossed her off my list for good.'

She pushed him away again and sat up. 'The little brown-haired cat! Did she admit that? Her fists clenched. 'I had a hunch he was playing around with another woman, but I never guessed it was Shelby.'

'She is somewhat deceiving in her working clothes,' he told her. 'Rather on the prissy side. But that's just a pose. When she takes off those horn-rimmed glasses and applies the war paint, the entire picture changes. She has the makings. Don't make any mistake about that. And it's my guess she's a very warm little number if she feels in the mood.'

'I suppose she was warm last night?'

'Warm enough to make me forget I had a bundle of money cached on me.'

She grunted and glared at him. 'Now I think you can understand what I've had to contend with. I'm not only married to an old stinker, but to a two-timing old heel as well. Believe me, Dan darling. With Clifton dead, the world will be a much better place to live in.'

'Never end a sentence with a preposition,' he chided. 'That's one of the points in grammar I remember from school.'

'To hell with your grammar. I talk the way I feel and not according to the rules. I like to say what I think in any way I choose to say it. A spade is a spade.' She reached across him and picked two cigarettes out of the box on the table. He found his lighter and lit them both. She leaned back against his chest, with her soft hair nuzzling his cheek.

'You asked me a little while ago what we would use for money if we were married,' she said. 'I'm not exactly a pauper. Clifton has given me stocks and bonds at various times. In fact he settled fifty thousand on me when I married him. That was part of my price. I don't know exactly, but I think I'm worth close to a hundred thousand.'

'That's your money,' Dan told her. 'I'm not the kind of jerk who lives off his wife.'

'I didn't think you were. The point I am trying to make is this. Clifton is an old man. He can't live much longer in any case. He has heart trouble and he keeps a small oxygen tank by his bed just in case. Frankly, I'd hoped he'd be dead by this time. Life with him becomes more difficult each day. And after what you've told me I'm sure he intends to change his will once he obtains the evidence he hired you to get. Don't you see, Dan darling?'

'See what?' He saw all right, but he had no intention of admitting it yet.

The death of Clifton McGowan had great and interesting possibilities. Dan was something of an opportunist. He had taken McGowan's offer and made the agreement with him because he had liked the sound of that hundred thousand dollars. He hadn't been making it anywhere near fast enough with the Keen Kleaners. McGowan's offer had sounded like a quick and pleasant way to make a large hunk of money fast.

He didn't care too much if the newspapers named him as Cleo McGowan's man. He didn't care if the people he knew called him a heel. With that much money in his bank account he could afford to tell them all to go swing on the garden gate. And that day for the first time in his life he had tasted the power and delight of what money could do.

The auto salesman had thought he was a big Texas oil man. The clerk at the haberdashery had been sure he was at least a multi-millionaire when he had glimpsed Dan's roll of bills. Even the owner of the Devonshire had fawned on him and made him think he was a VIP. It did something to his ego. Although he did not realize it himself, Dan Slick was not the same man he'd been the day before. He had gained confidence in his own ability, in his looks, in his outlook on life.

'How much do you figure your old man's worth?' he asked.

'I can tell you down to nearly the last penny,' Cleo answered with a throaty laugh. 'Including his life insurance which is two hundred thousand with a double indemnity clause, Clifton is worth a little over four million. If he should die accidentally, you can add to kiss them. They find that answers their questions.' another half million. He carries several accident policies and he never flies any place without taking out the limit on his life for the trip.'

'And all of it would come to you if he dies?'

'Every red cent,' she insisted. 'He hates charitable institutions almost as much as he despises the tax man. It's the one thing that worries him to death. He knows that when he dies, the way his will is drawn now, Uncle Sam will take close to half of it.'

'Seems as if there ought to be some angle he could work with a smart lawyer,' Dan suggested.

She shook her head. 'There isn't. His only chance is to form a trust with the income coming to me or some other benefactor and the principal going to the Red Cross or something like it.

Now you tell me that he doesn't intend to leave me a cent, that he wants to divorce me before he dies. I hate him.'

Her hands balled into fists and he could feel her whole body stiffen with her emotion. He tightened his arm around her, brought her face up close to his and whispered to her, telling her to relax. Then their lips met.

Dan pulled his mouth away, leaned over and kissed her.

'Maybe we ought to take another swim,' he suggested. 'That was fun the last time.'

'Why bother swimming?' she giggled. 'The help have all gone. My husband's in Frisco by this time.'

He laughed shakily.

'Sold,' he murmured. 'But first I need something to give me courage.' He reached over and picked up her brandy glass. With his free hand he filled it from the decanter. But when he started to drink out of it, she giggled and said, 'Me first.'

She didn't bother to sip it. She tipped it up and drained it in a single swallow. She handed it back to him. He refilled it, drained it himself and returned the glass to the table.

'I want some more brandy.' She reached for the snifter glass.

Dan poured it brimming full and watched her toss it down like it was nothing stronger than fruit juice. So far none of the stuff seemed to have much effect. She didn't talk with a lisp and her words made sense. On the other hand the last straight two fingers of brandy had done something to him. Ordinarily he could handle his liquor better than most.

She was leaning back now, against his arm, looking at him through narrowed eyes, the long lashes batting at him. 'You're a wonderful guy, Dan,' she purred. 'I love you. I want to be kissed.' Her voice raised a full tone in anticipation.

'Relax, sweetheart. I'm new at this sort of thing.'

With a shrug she sat straight.

She arched her back again, leaning as far against his arm as she could. 'Well?' she asked with a giggle. 'What are you going to do about it? Some men like to kiss. They find that answers their questions."

Chimes sounded somewhere in the back of the house. They chimed again insistently and Dan raged, 'Some one's punching the front door bell.'

Her eyes widened in sudden remembrance. 'Gosh! I completely forgot. It must be Carl. I told him he could come over before I made the date with you for dinner. What a nuisance! Just when we were having so much fun.' She leaned forward and kissed him quickly.

She slipped off his lap.

His nerves a shambles, Dan growled, 'What in the devil do you see in that type?'

As she headed for the living room, she turned and giggled at him, shaking a finger in his direction. 'You'd be surprised, Dan darling. Sometimes he's really wonderful company.'

CHAPTER FOURTEEN

DAN couldn't figure that one and after a moment's attempt to analyze it, he gave up, pushed the broken glass under the chaise longue, and straightened out the cushions.

Cleo came angling through the French doors with Carl Mabee in tow. He wasn't in dinner clothes this time, he wore pale gray slacks, a soft cashmere sport coat that blended with the slacks, gray suede shoes and a gray shirt with one of those Hollywood gimmicks that you wrap around your neck, then form into something that resembles an ascot. It was blood red. Dan decided that he might not be tough competition physically, but from the standpoint of what the well-dressed man should wear, he definitely was.

There was no doubt in Dan's mind about his having been marked with strange traits of character. He didn't walk when he moved, he skipped. There was, of course, Dan decided, the possibility that he could be bi-sexual. He knew there were men of such characteristics only he had never encountered one.

But there was one thing Dan was convinced of. Carl Mabee was no fool. He was a smooth character and a practising attorney. Clifton McGowan would hardly be stupid enough to pick out a fool for a lawyer. He could afford the best and he'd have it.

Mabee made no offer to shake hands and Cleo sent him to the kitchen for more ice and Scotch. 'I simply can't drink too much of that Amontillado brandy,' she announced with a giggle. 'It does things to me.'

Dan was of the opinion that she didn't need any kind of stimulant. It made him wonder again what she could possibly see in a man like Mabee.

As if she had read his mind, Cleo pinched his cheek. 'Jealous, I hope,' she whispered with a mocking smile.

'Jealous as hell,' he assured her. 'What do we do now? Sit around and get plastered while we wait for that little skipping crumb to leave?'

She looked at him through heavy lidded eyes, obviously enjoying his discomforture and trying to build his jealousy into a hotter blaze.

'That's not very nice, Dan darling,' she challenged. 'Carl isn't any different from you. Oh, I'll admit he's a little effeminate, but that's because he's always lived with his mother and for her. That's the reason he's never married. After his father died, which was a long time ago, Carl became her responsibility and she became his. She's a very delightful woman and quite young appearing. They seem more like brother and sister when they're together. We go to the symphony with them quite often. Carl's in his thirties so she must be in her forties, but you'd never guess it to look at her. She has naturally curly red hair. She wears it in a pony tail that's about the longest pony tail in existence. Reaches nearly to her waist. It makes her look like a girl in her teens at times.'

'Why tell me?' Dan grumbled.

Cleo laughed and shrugged. 'You'll undoubtedly meet her someday. I wanted you to be prepared. She is usually quite a shock to men. She's the type that attracts them like flies to honey. Then when they discover she is old enough to be their mother, they run like frightened hares.'

Mabee returned with a tray and placed it on the end table. He mixed highballs all around. After he had thoroughly covered Cleo's hours for the day, he turned to Dan with a smirk.

'Hear you have a new position with the boss, Slick? Some sort of a special investigator.'

Having just been handed the assignment the previous evening, Dan wondered how Mabee had learned of it and how much he knew about the agreement. Shelby Dorrance claimed she had typed the papers and Dan doubted if a man as astute as McGowan would permit his attorney, no matter how much he trusted him, to be a part of such a deal.

'You get your news fast,' Dan told him. 'The boss just appointed me last night and he left for San Francisco immediately after that. There must be a leak in the old man's office.'

Mabee chuckled. 'I have an excellent pipe line into Keen Kleaners, Slick. But don't worry. I shan't tell anyone else.'

He immediately ignored Dan and turned the talk into channels that were unfamiliar ground to a cleaner salesman. Dan finished his drink and decided he'd had enough. If Cleo wanted to carry on with Mabee where she had left off with Dan, that was all right by him. Only he had a hunch that this was one of those nights when she would shortly fold like she had the first time when the attack of asthma had knocked her for a loop.

Remembering the Great Dane which he hadn't seen since, he asked, 'By the way, Cleo. Where's Bren?'

She looked at him with one eyebrow raised, the other depressed, like she hadn't even known he was there until she head his voice. Mabee answered the question.

'Bren's in the kennel, Slick. Clifton is trying to find another home for him. With Cleo allergic to dogs he decided he might as well be rid of him, once and for all. Wouldn't like a nice Great Dane, would you?'

Dan shook his head. 'Thanks no. I've got enough troubles without adding a hound.'

He stood up, leaned over to shake hands with his hostess, told her he had to leave, that he had a lot of work ahead of him on the morrow.

Cleo was as cool as a summer night up at Lake Arrowhead. She didn't bother to rise. She looked at Dan as if he was something the Great Dane might have brought in from the alley.

Seething inside at the unexpected change in her, Dan stalked out, closed the front door behind him and climbed into his new Cad. Increasing his irritation was the sight of Mabee's small foreign car parked behind him so that he couldn't get out of the driveway easily. Dan settled that by releasing the brake on the Mabee car and shoving it back into the street. He backed the Cad out and drove off with the foreign car partially blocking traffic. Dan hoped a cop would come along and give him a ticket.

The Devonshire lobby was a tomb and there was no elevator attendant to take him up. Dan banged on the bell at the desk, heard steps behind him and turned to see the night clerk, whom he had never met, looking at him with the same half-questioning, half indifferent look he had seen on Cleo's face.

'The name is Daniel Slick,' Dan told him. 'I have room eight-oh-nine.' He accentuated the numerals. 'I should like my key and I should like some one to run the elevator if it isn't too much trouble.'

The clerk looked as if he didn't believe a word of it. He took his time going behind the desk, studying the register and making sure that there was a Daniel Slick. Then he reached the part of the register that named Dan's firm, and his whole behaviour changed. Dan was lifted to 8th floor by the clerk himself, asked if he wished anything from room service, and was ushered into his room like he was the Aga Khan himself.

Dan switched on the lights and stopped just inside the door. Some one else had been in his room besides the maid.

The room was a complete shambles. The sheets had been torn from the bed, the cushions tossed out of the chairs, his clothes dumped willy-nilly on the floor. All four drawers of the high-boy were open and his new shirts and ties and underwear scattered. Some one had even taken the time and the trouble to rip the band out of his hat.

Dan didn't have to guess what they were after. They wanted that twenty-five grand and the burglars were undoubtedly the same men who had sapped him up on Mulholland Drive. Some one must have followed him and found where he had lived. Yet if they had done that, they must have seen him enter the bank and even the safety deposit room at the rear.

Dan crossed to the phone, jiggled the receiver until the clerk answered. 'I thought you had a night watchman in this joint,' he ranted. 'If you have such a thing, where in the hell was he this evening?'

'Is something wrong, Mr. Slick?' The clerk's voice was tremulous.

'Come up here and see,' Dan told him. 'And bring the night watchman. I've been robbed, Mister, and some one's going to catch hell.'

Dan didn't have long to wait. The night clerk arrived with the night watchman, the maid, the assistant manager and the house dick, who looked as if he had just been aroused from a pleasant nap.

They took one look at the room and they all began to babble at once. They wanted to know what was missing, and Dan told them he hadn't had time to check, that he'd let them know in the morning. The maid re-did the bed, the watchman and the house dick examined the windows and the door. They finally came to the conclusion that the intruders had jimmied the lock, come in the front way.

'Where were you, John?' the assistant manager demanded of the aged watchman.

The old man grumbled, 'There's ten floors to this building. I can't be on all ten of them at the same time.'

Dan got tired of their bickering and accusing each other and drove them out. He hung his clothes back in the wardrobe, folded his shirts and returned them to the drawers in a more or less haphazard condition. He was too tired and frustrated to brush his teeth. He peeled off his clothes and went to sleep with the taste of lipstick on his tongue and the odour of Cleo's exotic scent in his nostrils. His clothes reeked of it.

He had left a call for ten-thirty. When the phone rang it frightened him so, he broke out into a cold sweat. With his mouth full of feathers and a grim resolve to leave Amontillado brandy strictly alone from then on, he went into his bath.

He was sure his stomach was full of grasshoppers and his head full of little men with hammers. He called room service and ordered a wild cow, a tall cold milk with two jiggers of bourbon in it and plenty of shaved ice. He ordered coffee, dry toast and a two minute egg. He wasn't positive he could eat the egg but he thought he'd give it a try.

The bourbon and milk steadied his stomach and he found the egg stayed down. He picked up the phone and called McGowan's office in the Sunset Building. Shelby's voice answered him and he greeted her pleasantly and without rancour.

'I was afraid you'd be sore,' she told him in a relieved voice

'Why should I?' he ridiculed. 'You and your friends got a couple of hundred bucks and package of funny money. I got thoroughly kissed plus a small lump on my noggin. And it was fun working over that little man with the rabbit's ears. Frankly, I'd like to try it again if you'll eliminate the lump.'

'I'm so glad you feel that way, darling,' she purred. 'After all we'll be working together at times, you know. You'll have to come to the office to report. And I still have a copy of the agreement. Someday you may change your mind and want to buy it.'

'Might at that, honey. No word from the big boss?'

'None as yet, but then I didn't expect any. He's not due back until the day after tomorrow. I'm free tonight, darling.'

'Have to check on my engagement book,' he chuckled. 'I'm a very popular man and you know why. Still have seventy-five grand to earn.'

'Why don't you quit while you're ahead? She's not in your class, darling. You and I could go a long ways on twenty-five thousand plus my savings.'

'Not with the big boss looking for us,' he advised. 'He'd spend his last dime trying to get that twenty-five grand back. No, for my money, until the old buzzard is in his grave, I think I'll follow orders. See you, sweetheart. Soon, I hope.'

Grinning, he replaced the instrument in its cradle and began to rearrange his clothes and place them back in order. He couldn't find anything missing and he came to the conclusion that the intruder was after the money. He couldn't remember the McGowan number and he looked for the directory. He found it in the small drawer of the night stand and he found something else that surprised him.

It was a .38 calibre revolver with a short barrel. It looked like the one the little man with the big ears had waved at him in Shelby's apartment. He broke it open and tipped the muzzle down. Six cartridges appeared. It had been fully loaded.

He looked for the serial numbers, but the only one he could find was on top of the barrel and that seemed to be a factory number. It was not a new gun and the make was one he had never heard of, a Richards and Harrington. He wondered if the prowler had left it in his room or if the man who'd occupied the room previous to his arrival had forgotten it? He started to pick up the phone and report it to the management, then changed his mind. The weapon might come in handy sometimes and it could hardly be traced to him as the owner.

He tucked the gun away in his top drawer under the shirts and returned to the phone. The maid answered at the McGowan home, then put him through to her mistress. Cleo sounded as if she had already had a couple. Her voice was as bright as a new twenty dollar gold piece. She told him to get over there and take her out to lunch.

Dan couldn't imagine anything nicer. He put on a pair of beige gabardine slacks, his new brown suede shoes and his cashmere sport coat. Maybe he didn't have the smooth looks of Carl Mabee, but he thought he appeared well dressed.

Promptly at twelve noon he rang the bell at the McGowans'. The maid let him in, not in the least surprised or shocked to see him. She told him that her mistress was not yet dressed and asked him to wait in the living room.

Dan helped himself to a smoke, walked to the plate glass sliding doors that looked out on the patio and the pool. He hadn't paid a great deal of attention to that area on previous occasions. He'd had too many other things on his mind. Much to his surprise the pool wasn't oval as he had thought, but kidney shaped. The bath house formed a protection from the property in back.

On both sides of the bath house were trees, on one side a huge old spreading oak, on the other citrus and deciduous. There were big yellow fruit on the one and Dan wondered if they tasted as nice as they looked. He was about to turn his back on the scene when he caught a movement that stopped him.

Carl Mabee came out of the bath house and walked to the edge of the pool. He was wearing Bermuda walking shorts and wool sox that reached to just below his knees. A white silk gaucho shirt was tucked into the shorts, stretched loosely across his skinny shoulders. The sun reflected from his dark and somewhat curly hair. It was longer than most men wear it, brushed back from the temples and over the ears.

When he moved it was with a dancer's feline grace, on the balls of his feet. Some sound made him turn. He vanished back into the bath house. Cleo appeared to the right, apparently coming from her bedroom. She was wearing a strapless sundress of lime-coloured cotton. She too vanished into the bath house.

The long minutes they vere gone seemed like an eternity to Dan. He didn't know why he should feel any jealousy over Cleo's affection for the attorney, yet he did and she knew and seemed to derive a certain satisfaction out of fanning the blaze.

When they finally reappeared, they were arm in arm. He was talking very earnestly and she was nodding and grinning. Suddenly as if she appreciated greatly what he had told her, she turned and faced him, her arms around his neck as she kissed him.

If Carl was strange, as Dan suspected, he didn't react to the caress like one. He coiled his thin arms around her waist. It was not the kiss of a celibate as McGowan had named him. There was fervour behind it and Cleo's response was positive.

Dan could feel his face and neck getting red with fury and he turned his back. Shocked, he stared at the figure facing him. McGowan had come into the living room silently, his feet deadened by the thick pile carpet, and he had apparently witnessed the scene as Dan had.

With a shrug that conveyed the idea that he had seen such scenes on many occasions, he said, 'I shouldn't let a man like Carl worry me too much, Dan. Their affection for each other is something that is difficult for a normal man to understand. I can assure you, there is nothing to it. I trust you have something to report in the way of progress?'

For a long minute Dan stared at him, his anger against Mabee dissolving while it slowly built up against the man who had hired him. He had determined that the next time he saw McGowan, he'd tell him what he thought of him. He took a single step toward McGowan and his two hands balled into fists instinctively.

'I ought to beat your Goddamned brains out,' he fumed. 'That was a really fast one you tried to pull, letting your secretary play the bait while she lured me to a nice lonely spot for a sapping. No thanks to you it didn't work'

He took another step in McGowan's direction. He couldn't remember ever having hated one man as much.

CHAPTER FIFTEEN

FEAR showed on McGowan's long face and he backed up, lifting one hand, palm toward Dan. 'Please, Mr. Slick. No violence. It was merely a test. That incident convinced me beyond a shadow of a doubt that I had picked the right man.' The laugh that followed was hollow-sounding and only faintly tinged with amusement. 'I must admit, however, that I should have enjoyed seeing you come crawling back with a tale of having been held up. It was quite clever of you to use the mails to protect your money, though it was taking a chance on the honesty of the postal clerks.'

Dan's anger simmered down and he grinned. 'I didn't think of the mails until later, McGowan. Actually the money was tucked behind the front seat of my car after the holdup. You have a most attractive secretary and she appears to be very loyal to you.'

McGowan looked not only surprised, but furious at Dan's news. Obviously the thought that a man of Dan's low intelligence could outwit three of his smart employees was highly irritating.

'Your pals didn't find anything in my room at the hotel either,' Dan added with a smirk, thinking he was adding insult to injury. 'But thanks for the gun. It might come in handy someday.'

'I'm afraid I don't understand.'

'Don't tell me it wasn't your goons that ransacked my room and left me a .38 revolver?' He studied McGowan's face and he could read nothing there but bewilderment.

'They had no such orders from me,' McGowan insisted. 'In fact I checked with bank the moment I was informed of your visit there. Although the manager refused to divulge the size of your bank account, he did say it was in four figures which convinced me that you had placed it in a safe place. Now suppose we stop this bickering. I want a report, Dan. I wish to see some progress quickly. And the sooner you get what I've asked for, the sooner you'll receive the balance of the payment.'

'I'd about given up hope of ever seeing that,' Dan told him.

'I gave you my word. I can assure you that the money will be paid the moment the evidence is in my hands. What are your plans? Can you arrange anything for today or tonight?'

Dan turned and glanced out the window behind him. Cleo and Mabee were still standing together in front of the bath house though they were no longer in close embrace.

'I've got a date with your wife to take her to lunch,' Dan said as he turned back. 'I doubt if I'll be able to arrange anything compromising in public. Cleo is no dumb bunny. I don't believe she suspects anything yet, but she might catch on fast.'

'How about another swim in the pool tonight?' McGowan suggested. 'That swim suit would photograph well.'

Dan shrugged. 'Have your photographer and your witnesses handy around say ten tonight. I'll try and arrange the pool scene. But be sure and douse all those garden lights just before you take the pictures. If you've got a good man he won't need flash. He can use infra red film and lights. Cleo won't even know the difference.'

McGowan apparently saw his wife heading for the house. He nodded and vanished almost as mysteriously as he had arrived. Dan was alone and smoking a cigarette when Cleo came through the patio door.

'Have you been here long, darling?' she asked with a small anxious frown. 'Nellie didn't tell me.'

'Long enough to see you with that creep,' Dan jeered, unable to control his jealousy. 'What the hell are you?'

'Jealous?' Her topaz eyes were bright with mischief.

Dan didn't stop to analyze his feelings. He only knew that his stomach was tied up in knots and the world looked as black as ink from where he was standing. He had wanted to slug the old man. The only thing that had stopped him was McGowan's age. He'd have liked to have torn Mabee limb from limb and thrown the pieces in the pool. He despised Cleo for what she was doing yet she was in his blood, she had broken down all his defences and he knew that if she curled her little finger at him, he'd jump.

The night before she had suggested that she could pay him more than her husband would for his services, and she had intimated that what she wanted done was nothing less than murder. Dan had recoiled at the first thought of it, but now that he had a gun that couldn't be traced, he had come to the conclusion that Cleo's idea had a lot of merit.

With McGowan dead and Cleo inheriting some two million or more, the seventy-five thousand that he had coming sounded like chicken feed. Cleo, he was sure, liked him as much as she did any man, and he was sure that he could give her more than a man like Mabee and he figured she realized it. She might be playing a cat and mouse game with Mabee. He was her husband's attorney and as such would have first information about the will and the old man's financial status.

All these things and more were revolving around in Dan's head as he said with a forced grin. 'You're damned right I'm jealous. I thought we settled that last night. I'm crazy mad about you, gorgeous. I don't want another man even touching you.'

She came in close to him, her face lifting, her two hands reaching up to encircle his neck. 'Then kiss me, you great big hunk of man.'

She was all woman, and in spite of the fact that her breath even this early in the morning had the unmistakable aroma of alcohol, he put his mouth to hers.

He was the one who had to come up for air and when he held her at arm's length and she asked with twinkling eyes, 'Satisfied, darling, that you're the man I truly love?' All he could do was nod foolishly.

She took his hand and said with an infectious giggle, 'I'm going to take you on the grand tour. Someday we might be living here together and you might as well know the floor plan now as later. Besides I want to show you my bedroom.'

'Boudoirs are my favorite haunts,' he chuckled. 'Lead on, my love.'

The house was not as large as Dan had suspected although it was roomy enough. There were only three bedrooms, one of which was used as McGowan's den and was panelled in walnut. The master bedroom that the old man slept in was unusually large with a huge bath and a pair of twin beds. Between the beds was a night stand with a telephone on the first shelf and instead of a bedside lamp, there was a small tank with a hose and rubber mouth piece.

'What's the tank for?' Dan asked curiously.

'Oxygen,' Cleo explained. 'Clifton had a heart attack a couple of years back. He keeps it there just in case. It seems silly to me. He's never used it. I try it occasionally when I have a bad hang-over. It's really fantastic the way it helps.'

There were sliding doors that looked out on the patio and Cleo remarked in an off-hand manner, 'Clifton sleeps in the bed furthest from the window. He's fearful of draughts.'

Testing her knowledge of her husband's whereabouts, Dan asked, 'By the way, he isn't home yet, is he? From Frisco, I mean?'

'Not that I know of,' she answered with a shrug. 'I believe he's due home tonight some time. Why?' She turned her glance on him, her eyes faintly mocking.

'Kind of hoped we might have a late swim tonight.'

Her eyes brightened. 'I don't see why not. If he does come home, he'll be exhausted from the plane trip and he'll go straight to bed. When we hear his car in the driveway, we'll simply turn off the lights and wait till he's retired and asleep.'

She took his hand again and led him from the master bedroom, through the den and the living room and across to her bedroom which also overlooked the patio and the pool.

This room was as large as the master bedroom and held a king size bed with a ruffled headboard. The wallpaper was lambs gambolling on a pale gray background. The woodwork was cream coloured. Adjoining it was a bath with a huge square tub and a separate shower stall and an extra large dressing room done in pink and soft shades of gray.

'This will be our room,' she simpered. 'After Clifton is dead.'

Dan put his arm around her waist and hugged her. 'I hope that day isn't far off, my sweet.'

Her face clouded and she said, 'I do hope you won't be angry, darling, I invited Carl to have lunch with us.'

Dan choked back the profanity that rose instantly to his lips. 'Sure, sweet,' he managed. 'That's okay. Anything you want is all right with me.'

She leaned over and touched his ear with her lips. 'I just knew you wouldn't mind. Come on. Let's have a drink. Carl should be back any minute.'

Back in the living room they had Martinis and a few minutes before one, Mabee walked in. He turned down the offer of a drink, said he'd wait till they arrived at the club. His car was too crowded for three so they used Dan's Cad with Cleo squeezed in between the two men.

The trip to the Beach Club was of no interest to Dan. Mabee was a good conversationalist. Dan wasn't. Mabee told amusing stories that brought laughter to Cleo's lips and made Dan grumpier.

It wasn't until they had finished drinks and the crab cocktails were served that Dan heard something that made him prick up his ears. Mabee was talking about Cleo's husband and what he intended to do.

'Clifton is going to change his will, darling. I'm to have a conference with him tomorrow. I know that I shouldn't tell you this. A client's conversation with his attorney is considered sacred. But you must realize that I have your interests at heart as much as Clifton's. I can't afford to argue with him. If it wasn't for his business I'd starve to death.'

Cleo put her fingers on Dan's arm, her muscles tightening, signalling him to listen carefully. 'How does he intend to change it, Carl?'

'The present will, as you know, leaves everything to you,' Mabee explained in a low voice. 'The new one will cut you off as far as it is possible under California laws. You will get no more than a widow's mite and possibly not even that. He's trying to find some loophole that will cut the community property out of the picture. There's only one thing I'm sure of, he won't leave a dime to any charity. I'm of the opinion that he has some sort of a trust in mind, whereby you'll receive a minimum of income with the principal going God knows where upon your death.'

Cleo's eyes turned on Dan, intent, and as probing as a surgeon's knife. They were no longer soft and warmly affectionate. They were cat's eyes, narrowed and sharp with speculation.

She turned her head slightly to look at Carl. 'What would happen if something—' She hesitated and began to choose her words with more care. 'What I mean is, supposing Clifton had an accident or say a heart attack before he signs the will?'

Mabee handed her a thin, somewhat sarcastic smile. 'You'd inherit the entire estate, of course. As far as we both know, Clifton has no living relatives besides yourself. But I wouldn't count on anything as fortunate as that. Sure, I know he's an old man, yet he's a damned healthy one.'

Once again her eyes returned to focus on Dan. He could almost guess what she was thinking. He knew too, that if she asked him to do it, he would. He'd do it if he burned in hell for it. He found himself hating and despising Clifton McGowan more than he had anyone in his short tenure of living.

The drive home was even worse than the one to the club. Dan decided that he might just as well have been a paid chauffeur. Cleo and Carl continued to discuss her husband, the changes in the will and what would or could happen to Cleo's finances.

'If he should decide to get a divorce, you might end up with no more than a small settlement that wouldn't amount to a hill of beans. He's a damned powerful man financially. I wouldn't say that he'd buy the judge, but I know he'd use every trick in the bag to cut you off with as little as possible. Unfortunately, I can't come to your rescue nor could I ever begin to support you in the style you've grown accustomed to. It's about all I can do to make ends meet with my mother to support.'

Cleo laughed throatily. 'I never had any intention of marrying you, Carl dear. You're sweet and I'm very fond of you, but—'

She shrugged and went no further. There was no need of any more talk. Her use of the word BUT conveyed a great deal, even to Dan, who felt a sudden sense of exhilaration, as if a heavy weight had been lifted from his shoulders.

'There is a chance if you sue him first,' Carl suggested in a faintly hopeless voice. 'It might give you an edge. I suppose you know he's been intimate with his secretary?'

'Guessed it, but I have no proof. What other grounds could I use?'

'Mental cruelty is the usual charge. It covers a multitude of sins. The women most generally get all the breaks in this state. But when you're up against someone as financially powerful as your husband, you're more apt to end up behind the eight ball.'

'Supposing he caught us in a compromising situation?' she suggested. 'Would that automatically leave me out in the cold?'

'Afraid it would.'

'But if I caught him?'

Mabee sighed deeply. 'It would help a great deal. At least you'd end up with a slice of alimony or a monthly stipend, the amount depending on the judge. The trouble is, I'm afraid you're not the type to gain much sympathy from a jurist.'

'Why do you say that?'

Mabee laughed. 'Too smart and sophisticated looking. Too much on the exotic side. Too much like the kind of a woman who'd use a man for all she was worth.'

'And no children,' she added with a shrug.

They reached the McGowan home and Dan parked on the street, remembering how Mabee's runabout had blocked him the last time. The three entered the house and Cleo went directly to the sideboard. She tossed off two fingers of brandy straight, then returned to the living room.

Joseph appeared like a genie coming out of a bottle and she told him to bring in a bucket of ice, highball glasses, and both Scotch and bourbon. Mabee excused himself with the statement that he had some work to do for her husband in the way of looking up some legal points in connection with the new will.

After he had left and Joseph had brought in the whiskey, Dan mixed a pair of highballs, but when he handed one to Cleo she promptly added another jigger to the glass, then sat down facing Dan.

'You heard what Carl said,' she began with her topaz eyes glittering. 'If we're going to do anything we'll have to work fast.'

Dan could feel a thousand tiny icy feet crawling up his spine. There were no longer any doubts in his mind as to what she intended to do. Clifton McGowan was going to die at someone's hands and before he could write a new will. Dan had more than a hunch she was intending to ask him to perform the operation. But if he did, what would he get out of it? That was something he wanted spelled out.

He took a long pull of his drink, set the glass on the end table and found that his hand was shaking. To steady it he lit a cigarette. When he looked up, his glance met hers. In her eyes he could see everything that he had ever wanted out of life, a lovely woman and more money than he had ever dreamed he could have. She had eliminated one competitor with the simple statement that she had never intended to marry him. That left Dan, and he was conceited enough to believe there was no other man.

'You tell me that you love me, that you're crazy about me,' he said. 'The feeling, I can assure you, is more than mutual. I never thought I could love any woman the way I do you. But if you're asking me to murder your husband, I want plenty of assurance that I won't be the patsy if the man with the badge catches up with us. Besides that, the sixty-four million dollar question is where and when and how do we eliminate this threat to your future and mine? I've no desire to end up either in the gas chamber or behind prison walls. We want to be able to enjoy; I'll not say our ill-gotten gains, because I think you're entitled to every penny you inherit.'

She was out of the chair in one fluid movement and perched on his knees. She held his face with her two hands while she crushed her mouth against his.

'Tonight,' she breathed against his lips. 'I've got it all planned out. No one will ever know darling. We'll do it while he's asleep. Bring your gun.'

CHAPTER SIXTEEN

DAN was startled. How did she know that he had a gun? he asked himself. No one else had seen it except the one who had left it in his room. Nor had he told anyone about it.

'What gave you the idea that I owned a gun?' he demanded. 'And why a gun anyway? They make a lot of noise. The sound of shots would be heard by your neighbours. They'd call the cops. Then where would we be?'

She leaned forward and kissed him again. 'You're the most naive man at times, Dan darling. There are lots of ways to deaden the sound of a revolver. Come on out in the patio. I want to show you something. I've been studying this a long time.'

She jumped from his lap and headed for the patio doors. Dan followed, his curiosity building up. They reached the west edge of the kidney shaped pool. She pointed to the master bedroom which was on the other side of the pool and partially hidden by trees and shrubbery.

'Clifton sleeps in that far twin bed,' she explained. 'He leaves the sliding door open for ventilation but with the screen door locked. He'll be thoroughly exhausted after his trip north. He'll be sound asleep and he won't even know there is anyone close. There is a burglar alarm, but it will be my job to see that it's turned off.'

Dan didn't believe that McGowan would be as tired as she hoped. He'd seen him earlier. He doubted if McGowan had even left town. He'd probably been spending the night with his secretary, Shelby Dorrance. Her flat would make a nice little hide-away. And this was the night when he had agreed to furnish McGowan the evidence he wanted. How could he arrange that and kill the old man in the bargain?

Yet the more he considered it the more he came to the conclusion that the only way to get what he wanted was to do murder. Cleo would have that to hold over his head for the rest of his life yet he could, if he wished, easily implicate her as an accessory. It seemed strange but he no longer gave Eddie a thought. She was something in the past, no more than a pleasant memory. This woman who stood beside him was what he wanted. And he no longer cared a great deal what he had to do to win her.

Then too there was the matter of some two million or more, money that he had never dreamed he could ever earn in a lifetime. He hadn't heard her complete plan, but he thought he could add to it, improve on it, and make it foolproof.

She turned to glance at him, frowning at his failure to answer her. 'What's worrying you, Dan darling? Surely you're not afraid?'

He put his arm around her waist, drawing her in close to his side. 'Just considering the angles, honey. Suppose you lay it out for me?'

He hardly heard what she was saying. Her question had shocked him out of his revery and forced him to a decision. No matter what her plan might be, they couldn't afford to have a photographer and witnesses around to watch a murder. In some way he had to stall McGowan.

Suddenly aware that she was telling him what he was to do, he said, 'Sounds too simple, honey. Go over it again.'

She gave him a quick and puzzled look, then continued. 'You'll come for dinner. Nellie and Joseph will be here to cook and serve. There will be just the two of us. Shortly after dinner, you will leave. There is a door in the tile wall behind the bath house. I'll see that it's unlocked. It leads into the alley that extends to Vernon Place. It is seldom used any more as most of the houses have garbage disposals and those that haven't put their trash and garbage out on the street. You can return that wav and no one will know the difference.'

'I need an alibi,' he interrupted. 'Where do I find one?'

'That's where I come in, silly.' She giggled ironically. 'I intend to spend the night with you at your hotel. If anything does go wrong, I'll swear that I was with you all night, that you never left your room.'

'You'd do that for me?'

She was putting herself out on a limb with that alibi and he knew it. If it ever had to be used, the press would crucify her. Yet it was the answer to his question. He was no longer uncertain of her love and loyalty. He swung her around and held her tight.

'It's a deal,' he told her. 'All the way.'

Later she shooed him out and he returned to his hotel. The clerk at the desk handed him a message with his key. He said, 'That party has called four times, Mr. Slick. She said it was very urgent.'

Dan took the elevator up to his room and called McGowan's office. Shelby answered and told him that the boss would like to see him as soon as possible.

'I think he has something to show you, Danny boy. Something you'll be terribly interested to see.' Her voice carried a lilt as if she was enjoying herself hugely.

'Okay, gorgeous,' he told her. 'I'll be there in a jiffy. Be seeing you.'

Dan took the elevator down, climbed back into his car, and headed for Sunset. Shelby was sitting primly behind her desk as he walked in. She gave him a bright and mystifying smile, called the boss on the intercom and told him that Mr. Slick had arrived.

She clicked it off and said to Dan, 'Go right in, Danny boy. But hold on to your hat. You're in for a real surprise. Do you know I never realised how photogenic you are. You should be in pictures.'

Dan scowled at her, unable to figure out what she was talking about and entered McGowan's office. McGowan waved him into the chair across from his desk and pushed a plain manila envelope toward him.

'Got some pictures I thought you'd like to see, Dan. Excellent ones too.'

Dan opened the envelope and drew out four glossy prints. He could feel his heart hammering against his rib cage as he studied them. They were pictures of Dan Slick and Cleo McGowan. They had been taken the first night he had dined with her and afterwards went swimming in the pool. There was one showing him holding her in his arms and kissing her. There was another one that was even more damaging from the standpoint of a divorce suit.

Dan looked up and stared at McGowan's triumphant yet cold eyes. He looked at the other two prints. One showed Cleo on the davenport in the living room. The other showed her sitting in Dan's lap. They were kissing. The picture even showed her apparent enjoyment. Her eyes were closed and the expression on her face told the rest of the story.

Disgusted as well as furious, Dan tossed the pictures back to the desk and lit a smoke. He leaned back in the chair. 'I don't need to ask when you got those,' he said with deceptive quietness. 'The question is, having taken them the first night we were together, why hire me and pay me twenty-five grand to get more?'

McGowan waved the question aside as inconsequential. 'The answer is simple, Dan. I had no idea they would turn out so well. If you will notice more closely they have been retouched.' He picked up the prints and stared at the ones that showed Dan and Cleo in the pool. 'My wife did have a swim suit on, but the photographer eliminated that. As you must have noticed.'

He returned the prints to the desk and he added with a faint smile of malice. 'This concludes the contract or agreement, you understand.'

'What about the remainder of the payment?' Dan asked softly, knowing that if McGowan did come through he would probably faint from shock.

McGowan ran true to form and expectations. 'You have a signed copy of the agreement, Dan?'

'You know damned well I haven't. But you did give me your word.'

'You are a most naive and trustful young man,' McGowan told him with a sneer. 'If you didn't guess then you must realize by this time that I have no intentions of throwing good money after bad.'

'And you think four glossy prints like that is enough to gain you an uncontested divorce?' Dan jeered.

'With the right witnesses to back them up,' McGowan replied, 'it will be no trick at all.'

In that moment Dan reached the decision that he had been trying ever since his last talk with Cleo to settle in his own mind. The idea of killing McGowan hadn't appealed to him in the least when Cleo had first broached it. That afternoon she had partially convinced him, yet not quite. There had been the fear of capture, the fear of what might happen to him and to Cleo if something went awry with their plans. Now suddenly he no longer cared.

To his way of thinking Clifton McGowan had already lived much too long. He had undoubtedly risen to his present pinnacle of success by using the skulls of his enemies to climb the ladder. Dan couldn't think of a single decent thing he could say about him. He was not only parsimonious and uncharitable, he was dishonest and would probably steal pennies from his own mother.

Dan pushed his chair back and stood up. He stared at the older man and instinctively and unaware of it himself, his eyes glittered and his big hands fisted into knotty clubs. McGowan hastily opened the switch on his intercom and reached into the top drawer of his desk for a gun, which he dragged out and held somewhat shakily pointing at Dan.

'Don't try any rough stuff,' he warned in a frightened and shaking voice. 'Miss Dorrance can get the police here in no time. You make one move and I'll shoot.'

Dan forced his hands to relax and he grinned. 'Mister,' he said. 'I wouldn't soil my hands touching you. You're not only an SOB, you're lower than a snake's rear end at the bottom of a thousand foot mine shaft. I've seen some lousy humans in my day, but brother, you ton them all. Too bad you've lived at long as you have. This topsy-turvy world would be a hundred per cent better off without men of your calibre.'

'You threatening me?' McGowan piped in his high voice. 'You heard that, Shelby. You can witness that statement,' he added into the intercom.

'Nuts to you.'

Dan was at a loss for any more words and turned his back and marched out. He slammed the door so hard behind him that the glass cracked, then fell to the floor with a tinkling sound.

Shelby Dorrance had her mouth open to say something, but when the glass broke, she held her fingers to her lips and she made signs to Dan that she'd like to meet him in the Pitcairn Room.

Dan grinned and nodded, then aloud he said, 'A good afternoon to you, Miss Dorrance. If there's one thing I need more than anything else, it's to take the bad taste out of my mouth.'

He slammed the outer door with the same vehemence, but either the glass was stouter or the door was more solidly built. It merely shook behind him.

In the Pitcairn Room down the street, Dan ordered a double Scotch over the rocks, fired up a smoke and waited for Shelby, wondering what she had on her mind. He found that he was not anywhere near as furious as he thought he should be at the loss of some seventy-five thousand, but then he told himself, he had never really expected to be paid the balance. Not since that first night when McGowan's goons had tried to san him and take away the down payment.

Shelby appeared in the ornate entrance with its South Seas, scrolls and puffed fish lights, spotted Dan and joined him in the booth and facing him. She ordered a Martini over the rocks and when the waitress had left to fill her order, she looked at Dan and grinned like an urchin.

'Hello, sucker! I warned you, remember? You should have accepted my offer. It's still not too late. You play around with that Cleo any longer and you're apt to find yourself either with a slug in your gut or eating cold mush behind bars.'

She opened her purse and pulled out a folded sheet of bond paper. She handed it across the desk to him. 'You want a copy of your agreement with McGowan, there it is. You want more, for a price I can get the original. I know how to open that safe.'

He glanced at the copy and shoved it back to her. 'How much?' he asked. 'Not for the copy. It's no good without his signature. The original might be worth a small bundle. With that I might be able to sue for breach of contract.'

She returned the copy to her purse as the Martini arrived. After the cocktail waitress had left, she said, 'I've been giving it a lot of thought, Dan darling. I wasn't kidding in the least that first night when I said you were mv kind of man. I got a small taste of you out there at Mulholland Drive and frankly, I was damned sore when those two goons arrived so soon. I figured they might have given us at least a half hour to neck.'

'You weren't so bad yourself,' Dan admitted. 'How much?' Then he added, 'When did you find out about the pictures?'

'This afternoon when they arrived. Clifton showed them to me. As I told you, you're real photogenic. Much more so than she is, the cat!'

'Tch, tch, baby. Cleo's all wool and at least a yard wide. Besides you're speaking of the woman I love and intend to marry.'

'You crazy or something?' Shelby blazed. 'She wouldn't marry a big lug like you. Especially now. Not after she finds out that hubby's got the evidence and that you were hired to do the dirty work. Be yourself, Danny boy. Wake up and be smart.'

'She knew what I was hired for the night those pictures were taken.' Dan answered smugly. 'I told her. It still made no difference.'

Shelby slapped her right ear with the heel of her right hand. 'Either my hearing's gone haywire or I'm listening to strange babble,' she remarked.

She finished her Martini in one gulp and started to get up. 'Long as you feel that way about that fraudulent broad, you might as well stew in your own juice. Heavens to Betsy! I thought you had all your marbles the way you out-foxed the boss's hired hands. I guess I was wrong. So long, sucker, and thanks for the drinks.'

With a laugh, Dan shoved her back into her seat. 'You didn't answer my question, baby. Maybe we can talk business. How much for the original?'

She sat down. She stared at Dan for a moment, then reached over suddenly and grabbed one of his big hands. She folded it into both of hers and looked at him intently, her eyes shining, the dimple in her chin winking on and off like a beacon.

'I guess beggars can't be choosers, Dan,' she said with a sigh. 'I'd like the whole works, but if I can't have that, I'll settle for part. If you'll marry me, I'll get the damned agreement for you for free. If you're still hepped on tying your star to one Cleo McGowan, then the price for the original is fifteen grand. Payable in advance.'

'Trusting little soul, aren't you?' he chuckled. He withdrew his hand from hers. 'In the first place I don't believe you can find that agreement. McGowan would hardly leave it in the office safe. It's more than likely in his safety deposit box, just as is my money. In the second place, honey child, although you're a lovely doll, I am as they used to say already bespoken for.'

She clenched her fists and glared at him. 'Okay, sucker. But don't say I didn't warn you. Why do you think the boss wants a divorce? Wake up, junior. He wants out because he knows what she is. When she isn't hitting the bottle she's trying to find some man to go with her.'

'And what's so terribly wrong with that?' Dan asked with a teasing grin. 'Those things have been going on for ages. You as much as intimated you'd tried it with your boss.'

She shrugged and slid out of the booth, standing there staring down at him, a puzzled look in her eyes. 'You can't be that dumb. You must have an angle.'

'Sure I've got an angle, baby.' He squirmed out of the seat and stood up beside her. He dropped enough bills on the counter to pay the check with a generous tip. 'It's an angle that I'm sure McGowan never considered. And it's worth some real dough, no chicken feed like a measly hundred grand.'

'I don't believe it.' She shook her head.

He took hold of her elbow and guided her to the street. 'Read the papers to morrow,' he suggested. 'I imagine it will be in the headlines. Good-bye.'

Dan left her and crossed to the parking lot where he had left his car. This was the night to end all nights and he crossed his fingers. He had either the world or a tiger by the tail and he wasn't quite sure which as yet.

CHAPTER SEVENTEEN

A S he pushed the starter button and heard the motor come to life, he wondered why he had told Shelby Dorrance as much as he had. In some ways it had been a foolish thing to do. At the moment he had thought she might pass the news along to McGowan and he had hoped it might worry him. Now he wasn't so sure that McGowan wouldn't take steps to protect himself. Dan had no desire to be caught in attempted murder by some of McGowan's hired goons. They played pretty rough.

Back at his hotel he relaxed on the bed and managed to sleep a little though his dreams were hardly conducive to rest. Mabee seemed to be in and out of them in a decidedly unpleasant fashion and Cleo first had Shelby's head on her body, then the gray and wrinkled old head of some woman to whom he had sold a cleaner months before.

It was close to being a nightmare and he came awake soaking wet with perspiration. He shaved and bathed, put on his navy blue suit and reached the McGowan residence at close to six-thirty. The maid admitted him, then Joseph took over to usher him into the living room where he found Cleo waiting for him. Much to his surprise she was dressed in a smartly tailored charcoal gray suit with a white blouse. Although it hardly seemed the correct thing to be doing in such a costume, she was wearing what Dan guessed was all her jewellery.

On her left hand was a square cut emerald the size of a dime exploded in a setting of baguettes together with a diamond and platinum wedding ring. Above those pieces on her wrist was a platinum and diamond wrist watch and a charm bracelet with a dozen or more jewelled charms dangling from it.

On her right arm were three other bracelets, one of emeralds and diamonds nearly an inch wide, one of diamonds in a twisted rope pattern, another of square cut diamonds and star rubies each one of which must have weighed at least ten carats. Below the arm on the third finger was a single diamond so big that it looked like it might be costume jewellery.

Joseph had Martinis mixed with small hot cheese canapes and after he had served and left the room, Cleo giggled and said, 'I noticed you staring at my jewellery, darling. Perhaps wondering why I was wearing so much? It's for a very good reason. Tonight I'm burning my bridges behind me. I'm moving out.'

Dan showed his bewilderment. 'But why, my sweet? You didn't mention that this noon when we talked. Where are you going?'

They were side by side on the davenport and she put her hand on his sleeve. 'With you, naturally. You have to have an alibi, remember?'

'But why this sudden change?' he asked.

'Don't you know?'

He nodded. 'You mean the pictures. Your husband showed them to me this afternoon. So help me, honey. I had no idea he was taking them. I swear, he didn't make the proposition until the next day.'

'I'm not blaming you, Dan. But can't you see? It's impossible for me to remain under the same roof with him any longer. After he called and told me, I packed all my clothes. We'll take the bags when we leave here and pick up the trunk and the other articles later. I hope your room is big enough to hold everything.

A woman can accumulate a lot of junk in ten years.' She smiled a little sadly.

'I didn't think it would be so hard to pull up stakes. Nellie's been with me for six years and Joseph for nearly five. They know my every whim. I do hope that after we're married and have our own home we can have them again. They are both such jewels.'

Dan patted her hand. 'You're going to have every-thing your little heart desires, honey. I'll see to that.'

Joseph announced dinner. Dan thought he looked a little sad, somewhat as if his life was falling apart too.

Ceo was very circumspect about her drinking. She had only two Martinis before the meal and a small snifter of brandy after-wards with her demi-tasse.

'Don't feel so bad about it, honey,' Dan advised. 'This is just one phase of your life that's finished. Tomorrow we start a new one. What time do you think your husband will be home?'

'Fairly early,' she answered. 'He has an appointment here with Carl. They are going over the new will together.'

'But he isn't going to sign it tonight?'

Dan was instantly apprehensive. If McGowan signed the will that night and it was witnessed, then there was no need to stick his neck out and kill the old buzzard. There would go his dreams of ever having two million dollars to spend.

Another thought struck him and he said, 'Just for the record, honey. I want something understood now. Any money you get from your husband's estate is yours. All I want and it's what I think I'm entitled to, is the seventy-five grand he promised and failed to deliver. Fair enough?'

'Don't be silly, darling.' Her eyes shone with affection. 'Without you the money would mean nothing to me. You're doing my dirty work for me. You're entitled to your share.'

Dan put his arm around her shoulders, then tipped her face up. He kissed her long and ardently. Suddenly he said, 'My room is no place for a couple of lovebirds to spend a pre-honeymoon. I'll call the Devonshire and tell them to make ready the bridal suite.'

'But, Dan darling—'

He laughed. 'Don't worry. They won't ask to see the marriage licence. I'll just tell them my wife arrived sooner than I expected by plane and that the single room is too small. They think I'm one of Clifton McGowan's big executives. There'll be no trouble at all. They'll be delighted to have us as their guests, especially after they take a look at you.'

'Flatterer!' she purred. 'I love you, darling. I love you so much it hurts. Don't ever turn against me. If you do, I'll kill myself. Even if you don't have a dime to your name I'll still adore you. I never knew what it was like to really love a man. Oh, I suppose I loved Clifton at first. He was generous and I was young and he gave me some lovely gifts. I'd never had anything before. A trunk and a rooming house. Occasionally a date with some stage-door and love-smitten Johnny. They all turned out the same. All they wanted was to go to bed.'

'Can't blame them for that, honey. I had the same feeling the first time I met you. Still have for that matter. Now suppose we get our time table straightened out. How are we going to know when your husband's in bed and asleep? The help doesn't sleep on the premises. You can't afford to let them call you anyhow.'

'That's simple, darling. Carl will call me at the hotel when he leaves. After that you can take over. Clifton will have a glass of hot milk and a sleeping pill. He always does. Inside of half an hour he'll be dead to the world, the house will be dark, and you can slip in through that door in the tile fence.'

'What about the burglar alarm?'

'I've already taken care of that. It works on a time clock. I changed the setting so that it would go on at the regular time, but go off an hour later.'

'I don't like this idea of having Mabee notify you when he leaves,' he complained. 'The less that creep knows the better. He's no dumb bunny. He might suspect something.'

'He suspects nothing. I had a perfectly valid excuse for wanting to know when Clifton was in bed. I told Carl that I didn't want to face him, but that I had to return to pick up the rest of my clothes. He knows about the photographs. Clifton told him too. He loves to gloat over anything like that, anything that would embarrass me. Clifton has a terrible mean streak in him. He adores trampling on people who try to cross him.'

'I've noticed that,' Dan answered wryly.

He glanced at his wrist watch. 'I'll make the call to the hotel and you get your bags. Have Joseph put them in the trunk compartment.' He reached into his pocket and gave her the keys. He leaned over and kissed her on the cheek. 'Back in a second, honey.'

He was walking on air. This was going to be a night to remember. For the first time since he had met her, she would be where he had wanted her from the beginning. He got the Devonshire on the phone, told the clerk what he wanted, and was assured the best of accommodations. They were sorry that the bridal suite was not available, but they had another suite equally as good. Dan told the clerk that they would be there inside of half an hour.

He returned to Cleo. She was in front of the mirror above the fireplace, adjusting a small cloche hat to her platinum curls. The front door was open and he could see Joseph placing the luggage in the trunk compartment.

Dan came up behind Cleo, put his arms around her slender waist, kissed her just below her ear. She turned around to face him, her arms going around his neck. He crushed his mouth to hers and they remained that way till Joseph coughed discreetly from the doorway.

Joseph looked as if he was about to burst into tears. Dan patted his shoulder, then reached into his trousers and brought out a roll of bills. He peeled off a twenty and stuffed it into the butler's palm.

'Soon as this is all settled, Joseph,' he said, 'you'll have another job waiting if you care to have it. You and Nellie both. You two have been grand.'

Joseph bowed and murmured, 'I wish you lots of luck, Sir. Goodnight. Sir.'

Dan helped Cleo into the car, closed the door, and moved around the convertible and climbed in beside her. Before he started the motor, he put his arm around her, brought her in close and kissed her.

'Just one for the road, honey. Do you know if it wasn't actually happening to me I wouldn't believe it? It's fantastic. A big lug like me and the most gorgeous creature in the world.'

'That's covering a lot of territory,' she giggled. 'But how I love it!' She snuggled up close to him and linked her hand under his right arm. 'I can hardly believe it myself. You're so right, Dan darling. The more I think of it, the more fantastic it seems. Tomorrow Clifton McGowan will be dead. Roasting in the fires of hell, I hope, if there is such a place. I never thought I'd be so glad to see a man die.'

He knew exactly what she meant. He had never before killed a man nor wished ill of him, but he found himself looking forward to the hour when he'd squeeze the trigger of that gun and see McGowan's body jump to the strike of the slugs. Never before had he bothered to hate a man. It had always been his belief that hatred did the hater more harm than the hated. If you disliked a person, the best thing to do was to avoid him.

He backed out, turned and headed for Sunset and the Devonshire. As they approached the Beverly Hills Hotel she said she was thirsty and why shouldn't they have a drink or two. More to humour her than anything else, he turned into the hotel driveway, gave the Cad to the parking attendant and went through the revolving doors. They found a quiet corner, ordered Scotch over the rocks and toasted their new found and continued happiness and success.

The cocktail lounge was crowded, but it didn't deter Cleo from demonstrating her affectionate nature. By the time they left he was as jittery as a cat on a hot tin roof.

The doorman removed the luggage from the trunk, a bellman took it up to their new room. The clerk told Dan that he had taken the liberty of removing Dan's belongings from the old room and placing them in the new one. With quick fear Dan realized that whoever did the moving must have found the revolver. He had left it under his shirts in the drawer. He started to tell the clerk what he thought of such effrontery, then as quickly changed his mind. The damage was already done and the clerk was only trying to be helpful.

The suite was large, expensive and more than luxurious from Dan's point of view although Cleo didn't seem to think it was anything special. After she looked it over, she remarked that it was somewhat on the dingy side and that the hotel must be second-rate.

Dan opened her luggage, set her overnight and makeup case in the small dressing room next to the bath, then went hunting for the gun. He found it under his shirts where someone had placed it, broke the weapon open and dumped the cartridges into his palm.

Cleo stood in the door and asked him what he was doing, and if that was the gun he expected to use. He told her it was, he explained how he had obtained it, and added that there was no way to trace it to him except possibly by the chambermaid or the bellman who had moved his clothes.

'They shouldn't have taken that liberty' she complained.

He agreed, pushed the cartridges back into the cylinder, and shoved the gun into his inside coat pocket. It bulged too much there so he transferred it to his belt and buttoned his coat over it.

'How are you going to leave here without the clerk or some-one in the lobby seeing you?' she asked with a worried frown.

Dan hadn't given that part a thought and he considered it carefully. The Devonshire not only had a night watchman and a house dick, but both of them knew Dan from the incident of the attempted burglary. If he took the back stairs, it was taking a long chance. The night watchman undoubtedly checked those and probably used them frequently.

He moved over to the window. The only other exit appeared to be the fire escape and if he used that he chanced some one see-ing him from one of the other rooms. Much to his surprise, Cleo had the answer.

'You men!' she nagged. 'I told you once before that you have to use your head to commit a perfect crime.' She crossed to the largest of her suitcases, opened it, and produced a wig, a false mustache, and a pair of dark Hollywood type glasses, as well as a black felt crushable fedora of Italian make.

'I was counting on you having something in the way of a coat that the management hasn't seen, or at least hasn't seen for several days. Something inconspicuous. Gray or brown.'

He remembered his old suit that he had worn as a salesman and that had been sent from the men's furnishing store after he had purchased new clothes. He got it out of the closet and showed it to her.

'Just the thing,' she told him. 'Now let's see how you look.'

He changed into the gray suit, tried on the false mustache and shook his head. 'Looks too phoney. I think we'll skip that.' He tried on the black felt hat, shaped the brim so that it tipped over one eye and looked at his reflection in the mirror. With the dark glasses hiding his eyes he decided it was unlikely he would be recognized.

He pushed the gun into his belt, buttoned his coat over it, glanced at his wrist watch. 'How long do you suppose Mabee will be in conference with your husband?' he asked. 'This waiting to kill a man is nerve racking.'

'Clifton retires soon after nine as a general rule. We should hear from him any minute.' She moved close and put her arms around his neck. 'Scared, Dan darling? There's no need to be. It will be easy.'

'I don't know whether it's fear or nerves,' he told her as he put his hands around her back. 'I only know this is the first time I ever started out to kill a man. I've got a funny feeling in my stomach, sort of like it was full of jumping grasshoppers. First I feel hot, then I feel cold.'

'That's normal,' she giggled. 'You'll be all right when it's over. And there is absolutely nothing to fear. The burglar alarm is taken care of and the gate is unlocked behind the bath house. There will undoubtedly be a night light in Clifton's bath and possibly one between the beds. You can reach the bedroom by skirting the fence. You'll be in back of the trees all the way. If you're careful, no one can possibly see you from the house.'

'You said there wouldn't be anyone in the house,' he worried.

'There won't be as far as I know,' she insisted. 'I'm telling you all this just in case. I don't want you to take any chances. And remember this, up near Clifton's room on the flagstones is a chaise longue with a pair of cushions. Take one of those cushions into Clifton's room with you. Use it to deaden the report of the revolver. Once you've killed him, return the same way you came in. No one ever uses that alley any more and there are no dogs close to it.'

He held her tight and put his mouth to hers, gaining courage from her nearness and the thought that once it was finished, they could be together for always.

The buzz of the house phone startled them. Cleo picked up the instrument, said 'Hello' in a throaty, excited voice, then with a simple 'Thank you' she returned it to its cradle.

She turned around to stare at Dan, her topaz eyes glittering with turbulent excitement. 'Carl left the house more than ten minutes ago. Clifton was undressed and taking his sedative and hot milk. By the time you reach there he'll be dead to the world. He won't even know what hit him.'

As if fearing he might suddenly change his mind and back out, she returned to his arms, her lips demanding.

'Be careful, darling,' she whispered. 'If anything goes wrong I think I'll die.'

'If anything does go wrong,' he replied, 'you won't be the only one who dies. Little Danny Slick will be spending his last hours in the death house up at San Quentin. So keep your fingers crossed.'

CHAPTER EIGHTEEN

CLEO followed him to the door, closed it behind him, and Dan walked leisurely to the stairs. He walked down three flights, then took the elevator the rest of the way. The boy looked at him somewhat curiously, then apparently decided that the man in the dark glasses was either some would-be movie actor or someone aping the Hollywood style of wearing dark glasses at night, so that the public might think he was a celebrity.

The lobby was empty and the clerk didn't even turn around as Dan slipped by and reached the street. The doorman said good evening and Dan, after answering in a disguised voice, walked rapidly away in the direction of his car.

He breathed a little easier after that experience, but he soon found that he was sweating profusely. He seldom wore a hat and the one Cleo had brought was a little on the tight side. He removed it and placed it on the seat.

When he finally reached the residential area where the McGowan's lived on a hunch Dan circled the block, passed the alley that extended into Vernon Place and driving slowly stared into its dark and gloomy depths. He would much preferred to have driven up to the front door and rang the bell and had been admitted. He didn't like this idea of skulking down dark alleys. Some nosy neighbour might see him, call the police, or even take a pot shot at him. Dan had no desire to be on the receiving end of a bullet.

His hands felt cold and clammy and the grasshoppers were back in his belly. He had an insane desire to forget the whole thing, return to his rooms at the Devonshire and tell Cleo all bets were off. It was the thought of her and the two million dollars as well as his hatred of the man he intended to kill that drove him on.

Clifton McGowan deserved to die, he told himself. He had already lived too long. And Dan had no remorse nor did he think he would feel any when the industrialist died at his hands. He had every intention of shooting the old man in the gut so that he would die in pain and not too swiftly.

Parking finally in a spot that was handy but not suspicious, Dan slid from under the wheel, studied the street in both directions, then silently ran into the darkness of the alley. He stood just off the street for a long moment, letting his eyes get accustomed to the alley's blackness. He would have liked to have had a flash, but he was afraid such a beam of light might attract the attention of a neighbour or a cruising police car.

With his eyes finally accustomed to the darkness, he began to feel his way along the fence, slowly and painstakingly so that he wouldn't trip over any rubbish that might be lying in his path. Several times he stopped to listen, for every sound seemed magnified to his taut nerves.

Off somewhere and at least a block away, a dog set up its insistent howling. Somewhere a motor horn blared and from another direction Dan heard the whine of a starter followed by the sound of a motor revving to life.

He felt the gate finally, found the knob and slowly turned it. The gate opened soundlessly under his pressing hand, and with a sudden impulse he slipped inside, closed the door in back of him and stood with his back to it, his ears trying to sort the various sounds around him. He thought he heard the bang of a door or perhaps the scrape of furniture somewhere ahead of him and he turned quickly to make a hasty exit if the McGowan home had any occupants.

The noise, faint as it had been, was not repeated and Dan sucked in his breath in relief and started to move ahead. Using his hand to follow the stucco wall of the bath house he slowly skirted its rear, moved carefully between a pair of citrus trees that were heavy with grapefruit and reached a spot where he was hidden but could see the main dwelling and its outline.

The kidney shaped pool stretched in front of him, the water looking dark and unappetizing under the clouded sky. Around it were the dark shapes of the chairs and chaise longues, the sun pads looking like human beings in their rectangular blackness. He could see no lights in the main part of the house, he could hear no movement.

Gathering his slipping courage he headed for the spot where the master bedroom was located. Once he barked his shin on a lawn sprinkler and he cursed silently as the pain shot up his leg and took the time to rub it a little.

He came from between two trees and found himself in front but to one side of the master bedroom. The sliding door was open, but the screen was closed. Almost directly in front of him was the chaise longue Cleo had mentioned with its twin pillows.

As if someone might grab one before he did, Dan reached out and scooped one up and tucked it under his arm. He removed the gun from his belt, cocked it, and began to steal forward, determined now to get the job done before his nerves cracked and he fled in panic.

He was worried about opening the screen door till he reached it and found that it was unlocked. Not until then did he see McGowan. He was lying in the far twin bed. His face was pointed in Dan's direction and his head was partially raised by two pillows. Dan could see the mouthpiece of the inhalator on the night stand close to his head and within easy reach of his hand should he feel an attack coming on.

The long thin and wrinkled face looked as if it had been bleached to the whiteness of a corpse in the morgue. The tiny night lamp that was fastened into the wall plug just under the top of the night stand was too feeble in candlepower to reach up much beyond the top of the bed.

Slowly and painstakingly Dan slid the screen door back until the aperture was wide enough for him to slip inside. Here again he paused and listened, the hairs at the back of his neck stiffening in gnawing apprehension that something was wrong with he picture although it was exactly as Cleo had told him it would be.

There was no doubt in his mind but that McGowan was deep in slumber. The carpet under his feet was thick enough to deaden any sound his feet might make and in spite of his fears, he kept telling himself that there was nothing to worry about. McGowan would probably never know what hit him. Dan found himself wishing that the old man might see and recognize his killer before he died.

With an effort he gathered his courage and stepped closer to the bed. He raised the pillow to cover the muzzle of the gun with it, suddenly changed his mind. He wasn't sure what a pillow might do to the trajectory of a bullet. He wanted to be sure that every bullet found its target.

That was when he saw McGowan's eyes. They were wide open and staring at him with the hypnotic effect of a reptile. Dan's reaction was instinctive and born of fear and hatred.

'Take this along with you,' he snarled, as he pulled the trigger three times, seing each bullet strike into the coverings that hid McGowan's body and sure that each one had gone home.

Suddenly aware of the magnitude of his deed and the possible consequences to his own good health if he didn't get out of there fast, Dan turned.

It was a turn that never stopped. Something came out of the blackness like a pile driver and hit the top of his head with a sickening thud. The turn became a slow whirl, then a spin until finally there was nothing beneath but an empty void into which he was falling and falling with no strength in his arms left to even reach out and try and stop his momentum.

After that it became a series of nightmares that seemed to have no conscious beginnings nor endings. His Uncle James from Texas appeared in one of these, holding a shield in front of him and carrying a long sword like the Crusaders had used. He heard voices around him, but the words were unintelligible and the pain in his head incessant, frightening and never ending.

At one time he thought he detected a familiar voice and when he opened his eyes to stare, he recognized Norton who had taken over his job as branch manager of the Keen Kleaners.

'What in the hell are you doing here?' Dan asked.

It was all he said. Norton's face dissolved, Dan closed his eyes and drifted into another troubled sleep that was peopled with strange characters, some of whom he remembered from his youth, some of whom he could not recognise.

Occasionally he heard the clanging bell of a trolley, the sound of a motor horn, or the distant and eerie wail of a switch engine. He could hear voices around him and he could on rare occasions catch a word or two that made no sense.

'Temperature's normal and so is his pulse. I'm sorry, Captain. I have no idea how long it will be before he will be lucid enough to understand you. There is a very definite improvement. I can say that. He has a good appetite, but as you can see there is no sign of intelligence in his eyes.'

Dan heard a deep sigh then the words in a deeper voice. 'Tough luck for me, Doc. If I could just get something out of him I think I could crack this case open wide in no time.'

'I fail to see why you're worried. This man was caught red handed so to speak. The gun matches the slugs that were taken out of the dead man. That man Mabee claimed they were waiting to catch him in the act of murdering, but that they arrived too late to stop him. He had threatened his victim before, according to the secretary. By the way, Captain, they are both very attractive women.'

Dan heard a booming if somewhat mocking laugh. 'You're telling me, Doc. That McGowan female is really something. I kind of liked her as a blonde when I first met her two months ago the night of the murder, but she's something extra special now that she's a red-head. With those yellow eyes, man oh man! This poor devil doesn't know what he's missing.'

'And just as well. There's not much future left for Daniel Slick. The gas chamber in all probability and certainly nothing less than a life term in San Quentin.'

The voices faded away and Dan slept. He had other visitors some of whom he knew about, but none that he recognized until the day he heard a soft and tremulous voice saying over and over again, a voice that was tear-filled, 'Oh, my poor darling. My poor darling.'

Dan opened his eyes and stared. 'Eddie,' he whispered. 'Hello, Eddie. Gosh, you look like a million dollars.'

'Dan!' she cried. 'Oh, Dan darling. I've been so worried. You recognized me. Now I know you're going to get well.'

The pains in his head started again and he closed his eyes. Unconsciously his hands clenched and remembering a previous experience, the girl moved swiftly out of reach and motioned to the male nurse who came quickly and silently watchful.

The pains subsided and Dan reopened his eyes, letting his muscles relax. But the girl standing at the foot of his bed was no longer Eddie Goes. It was Shelby Dorrance and he saw the way the light from the big window behind her shone through her reddish-tinted hair and made it look like it was filled with burning embers.

'Hello, Shelby,' he murmured. 'How's that old buzzard you call your boss? I hope by this time he's frying in hell.'

Once again the sickening thud of pain struck through his head and he screamed, afterwards hearing his own voice echo and echo up and down the room and wondering why.

Each day was much like the previous one. He was aware that some one in a white jacket brought him his meals at regular intervals, yet it seemed to him as if there was never enough. He had no idea where he was nor why. His past life except for brief flashes of time was an almost total blank. People came to visit him, but he knew none of them.

They gave him the daily papers to read and there finally came a day when he was allowed to sit up. He stared around him at the unfamiliar surroundings. He had been in a Navy hospital once and this place seemed similar in some respects. But he couldn't understand why they had so many male attendants and so few females.

There were fourteen other men in the ward and they treated Dan as if he were a pariah, though no one said anything to him. The attendants were indifferent, answering his questions in monosyllables. Each morning the physician in charge examined him, stared into his eyes with a tiny light, felt the back of his head.

A big heavy set man arrived one day with another younger man. He introduced himself as Captain Luke Dollar of Homicide. The man with him was Sergeant Drake. He said he'd like to ask Dan a few questions.

Dan looked at him blankly. 'Sure,' he said.

'What's your name?'

Dan frowned and tried to remember. Nothing came out of his memory and he said, 'Sorry, Mister. I can't seem to remember.'

'Do you know where you are?'

Dan glanced around him, managed a thin smile. 'Looks like the Navy Hospital at Dago.' A frown clouded his forehead. 'That's funny. I thought they discharged me as cured. That was a long time ago. Say, Mister, how's my buddy Joe?'

The sergeant looked at Captain Dollar and shook his head. 'Nothing seems to register yet. Or maybe he's putting it on.'

Dollar said, 'Not with eyes like that, Hank. The doc said he didn't think it would work yet.' He sighed and smiled in a friendly way at Dan. 'Be seeing you, Slick.'

Dan's eyes opened a little wider and he asked quickly, 'What did you call me, Mister?'

Dollar said, 'Slick. Daniel Slick. That's your name according to our records.'

'Not a bad name,' Dan remarked. 'I kind of like it.' He relaxed back on the pillows and closed his eyes. 'Slick,' he murmured over and over again as if he was trying to fix it permanently in his mind.

Later that day he had another visitor. He heard a woman's voice and the name Dan called. He opened his eyes. The young woman stood at the foot of the bed. She was wearing a plainly tailored charcoal gray suit with a white blouse that had lacy pleats down the front. There was a small flowered hat on her hair. The hair was an almost incredible shade of black and the eyes beneath it seemed as dark.

'Don't you know me, Dan?' she asked.

Dan looked at her face, his eyes narrowing as he tried to dredge something out of his memory. Finally he said with a broad grin, 'I don't know how I could ever forget a good looking doll like you, honey. Something must have happened. Your kind aren't a dime a dozen. You're something extra special. Mind if I ask you your name?'

Her face had coloured slightly under the probing quality of his gaze and she said, 'Eddie Goes. Dan. We used to work together. You were my boss. When you were the branch manager of Keen Kleaners.'

'Did I ever kiss you?' he asked.

She nodded. 'Several times. You asked me to marry you, but I didn't have enough sense to say yes.'

'Good thing you didn't.' he told her with a heavy frown. 'You wouldn't want to be tied to a cripple.'

'That's where you're wrong. Dan. I never knew how much I loved you till you walked out on me.'

'I must have been out of my mind, honey. Why would I do a thing like that?'

'There was another woman.'

He shook his head slowly from side to side. 'That doesn't make any sense. What did she have that you haven't got?'

Eddie's lips tightened. 'She had red hair and a husband with a lot of money whom she wanted to be rid of. You played right into her hands. Oh, Dan!' Tears silvered the long dark lashes and she brushed them off with the back of her hand. 'I still don't believe you did it. I just can't. Dan darling. You were tough and hard, but you were never that bad. Something is terribly wrong.'

Suddenly his head began to ache. The pain came in great throbbing surges, like huge combers breaking against the rocky shore line. For some reason it reminded him of the day that he and his friend Joe had lain in the surf off Tarawa, their rubber-encased bodies hidden just beneath the surface, each of them carrying a demolition bomb that their commander hoped would make landing easier for the first wave of marines.

There had been no pain then, only a dullness and silence around them, broken by the occasional loud sound of a shell exploded on the beach, a sound that bounced off the surface of the water, yet could be felt like the slap of a heavy hand.

Unconsciously his hands clenched and his body twisted and writhed. Eddie signalled one of the attendants who came swiftly. But before he reached the bed, the pain had subsided and Dan had opened his eyes, seeing the girl for the first time, his memory flooding back in waves that turned into nausea.

He looked at Eddie, his eyes racked with the pain of his thoughts. 'Did I kill the old buzzard?' he asked.

She didn't have to answer. He saw her nod her dark head, he saw the ache in her eyes, the drooping lips that made her look as if she might burst into tears any moment.

'Sorry, Eddie,' he mumbled. 'I sure as hell must have botched everything.'

CHAPTER NINETEEN

THEY let him sleep the rest of the day and all that night. Soon after he had finished his breakfast. Captain Dollar was back with Sergeant Drake and another man whom they said was from the District Attorney's office. They helped him out of bed, a nurse put a bathrobe around his shoulders and they walked to the elevator.

They took him down to the third floor and into the Homicide Division. They squeezed into an interrogation room, sat Dan at a table and when the stenographer had readied himself with notebook and pencil, they began to ask questions.

Dan told them how he had left the Devonshire and the disguise he had worn. He explained how he had prowled the alley and how the gate was unlocked. Afterwards he had crossed the yard to the sliding windows, silently opened the screen door and stepped inside. Clifton McGowan had been lying in bed facing the window. Dan had seen McGowan's open eyes staring at him and in sudden panic and anxiety to get the job done, he had shot McGowan three times. After that he couldn't remember anything.

Captain Dollar said, 'When the boys from homicide arrived, you were on the floor with a bashed-in head. I don't suppose you saw who hit you?'

Dan shook his head and Dollar said, 'It was Carl Mabee. He hit you with a wooden ice mallet. One of those kind you use on a canvas bag to make crushed ice.'

'Who helped you, Dan?'

Dollar jabbed the question at him unexpectedly. Dan opened his mouth, then angrily closed it. Until he knew more about what happened after McGowan's death he didn't intend to implicate Cleo. She'd spent ten years married to an SOB who deserved to die. He and Cleo might still have a chance to enjoy that fortune the old man had left her.

'Who was in the bedroom when the police found me?' Dan asked.

Dollar enumerated them from a list he picked out of his pocket. 'Carl Mabee, McGowan's attorney: Joseph Teller, the butler; Nellie Sands, the maid; and Mrs. McGowan. Four witnesses, Dan. You're not telling all the truth. If you can't come up with something the jury and the judge will most likely hand you the gas chamber. The least you can get is a life sentence. Why hold out on us? It will come out sooner or later. Did Mrs. McGowan hire you to do the job?'

Dan laughed mockingly. 'What a stupid question! Not that I don't believe she's glad he's dead. He was a real stinker. He hired me to get evidence so he could divorce his wife, then shows me pictures he's taken the first night we were together. What a lousy trick! We made an agreement. Then after he pays me the money he sics a pair of goons on me to try and take it away. Believe me, Captain. I don't regret killing that bastard in the least. He deserved to die. He'd already lived too damned long.'

'Why did Mrs. McGowan move into the Devonshire with you the night of the murder?' Dollar demanded sharply. 'Sounds like collusion to me.'

'McGowan had kicked her out,' Dan answered. 'Besides we were in love.'

There were more questions, but Dan kept his mouth shut. He was afraid he had already said too much. Dollar asked him if he wanted a lawyer. Dan said he didn't think so. At least not yet. There were a couple of angles that he wanted to consider.

He thought about them far into the night after the attendant had taken away his dinner and the lights went out. Why had Cleo been in that master bedroom he kept asking himself. She was supposed to be at the hotel. She was to be his alibi. There was something screwy about the entire deal, but Dan couldn't fit the pieces together. He still refused to believe the truth, that he had been played for a sucker, that Cleo had never intended to marry him. She had just wanted her husband murdered.

The more he went over it in his mind, the closer he came to the realization that he had been framed, framed by a beautiful female and a damned crumb. The two of them had to be in it together. There couldn't be any other answer. But what did Cleo see in that Carl Mabee? She was a healthy female. It was the one puzzle he had never been able to solve since he had first seen Mabee and Cleo together.

That embrace and kiss had been more than platonic. Cleo had reacted as much to the caress as she had to Dan's. Mabee had too.

Two weeks later they moved Dan from the hospital ward to the jail. They gave him a cell, but with bullet proof and unbreakable glass partitions, Dan could see many of the other inmates. Although his legs were still weak, he was growing stronger each day and more worried as to the ultimate outcome. The guard knew nothing and no one else came to see him.

Dan kept hoping that Cleo would appear, if only for a brief moment, just long enough to reassure him. But all Dan could do now was wait; wait for the authorities to gather the evidence that would make conviction certain; wait for his trial to be put on the calendar.

From the moment when his memory had returned and he had heard there were four witnesses to McGowan's murder, Dan had become resigned to his fate. Captain Dollar had told him that the judge might let him off with a life sentence. Certainly nothing less, though perhaps with a chance for parole.

His breakfast was finished, the tray waiting to be picked up by the turnkey. Dan was smoking a cigarette, gloomily contemplating his future. Even Eddie hadn't reappeared to console him. Not that he blamed her. He had treated her pretty shabbily after asking her to marry him.

He heard Boaker's feet making that slap-slap sound on the floor. You couldn't mistake either Captain Dollar's or Boaker's feet. Dollar walked on his toes. Boaker came down on his heels first in a kind of shuffling fashion. The heels were rubber and made no sound. It was the sole slapping on the treated concrete floor.

He reached Dan's door. Dan noticed that he was carrying Dan's old gray suit, the one he had worn the night of the murder, the one they had found him in when they had dropped him on a stretcher and put him under arrest.

'What gives?' Dan asked curiously. 'Court in session?'

Boaker lifted and dropped his round shoulders as he unlocked the door and stepped inside. 'Don't ask so damned many questions,' he grumbled. 'Put on your clothes. Captain's orders. Some kind of a conference in the D.A.'s office. Captain Dollar said he'd be here at eleven. You got plenty of time to dress. You'd better shave too. There's a safety there with the clothes.'

'Aren't you afraid I might cut my throat?' Dan chided.

'Far as I know no one gives a damn if you do,' Boaker answered. 'You feel like dying that way, go ahead and try it. I got news for you. It's messy as hell and someone will find you before you pass out.'

The suit had been pressed and the white shirt laundered. Captain Dollar was right on time. Boaker unlocked the door.

When Dollar made no motion to put on the handcuffs, Dan jeered, 'What about the cuffs, Captain? I'm a suspected killer, remember?'

'Let me worry about that,' was the reply.

They left the new jail with its huge windows and the controversial faceless and bronze statue that looked down on the street and well kept lawns. Later they entered the Hall of Justice and Dan and the Homicide captain were lifted to the offices of the District Attorney.

Much to Dan's surprise Cleo McGowan had the chair facing him at the conference table. She glanced once at him when he came in without a flicker of recognition, then kept her eyes averted after that. Her hair was red again, long and coiled into a small chignon at the nape of her neck. A green hat that looked somewhat like an inverted salad bowl hid most of her hair. A worried frown tugged at the smooth lines of her forehead and the topaz eyes were deeply ringed and watchfully wary.

Carl Mabee sat next to her. Each time he looked at Dan he scowled. A plain clothes detective sat on each side of Dan. Captain Dollar sat at the west end of the long table, flanked on each side by a pair of men from the crime lab.

The District Attorney sat at the other end, an assistant attorney on one side, a stenographer on the other. There were stacks of papers on the desk, exhibits from the crime lab, including the gun Dan had used to shoot McGowan.

Dan's eyes caught the D.A.'s glance. That one look convinced Dan that in the eyes of the District Attorney, he was riff-raff.

'Smoking is permitted,' the District Attorney said by way of opening the proceedings. 'All right, Captain Dollar. This is your show.'

Dollar shuffled the papers on his desk, found what he wanted and said, 'The first thing 'Im going to do is read the transcript of Daniel Slick's confession to the murder of Clifton McGowan. It will not be necessary for the stenotyper to copy it as copies have been furnished to the District Attorney's office.'

To Dan, Dollar's voice droning on and on, telling what Dan had said, seemed unreal and something like a dream. Dan glanced at Cleo. Her face had a strained look and she was staring at her hands; hands that were held tightly clamped together in front of her on the table. Dan was sure she was deeply conscious of his gaze and she was aware that everyone else was staring at her. But she neither raised her head nor lifted the shutters from her yellow eyes.

Captain Dollar's words were nothing new to Dan. They had been Dan's originally and he told as simply as he knew how, how he had followed the alley to the gate, slipped inside, crossed the yard, and finally shot McGowan, then had turned to run, only to be slugged by someone.

Being a lawyer, Mabee seemed to think he had rights and he interrupted the proceedings with the statement that the entire conference was illegal and totally unessential. 'I ask you, gentlemen. Look at my client, Mrs. Clifton McGowan. Isn't it enough that she has suffered untold anguish and sorrow at the hands of this—this unprincipled ruffian? Look at him. I beg of you. He feels no remorse. He has even gone so far as to admit to the Homicide Captain that he's glad he killed the old bastard. Those were his very words.'

Dan looked at Mabee and grinned. 'I'll say it again, Mabee, if you'd like to hear it. Clifton McGowan had already lived too long. And I'm damned sure his death pleased you as much as it did me.'

'That will be enough from the prisoner.' The District Attorney's voice batted Dan into silence. 'I am willing to admit that this procedure is highly irregular, Mr. Mabee. But so are the facts in the case as presented to me by Captain Dollar. Continue, Captain Dollar.'

There was the faintest of smiles on the Homicide Captain's face and Dan caught it and wondered. For the first time since his arrest and the return of his memory, a faint hope began to build inside of him. Luke Dollar, he knew from what he had heard, was a smart cop and one who never took circumstantial evidence without a thorough investigation. He had told Dan that he wasn't satisfied with what he had found out, that he didn't think the whole truth was out.

Dollar placed the paper back on the table and picked up another report. 'This may come as a shock to some of you here, but here is the report of the coroner and the autopsies. Clifton McGowan did not die from gunshot wounds inflicted by Daniel Slick'

'What did he die of then?' Mabee demanded with a faint sneer.

'He died of carbon monoxide poisoning and he had been dead for at least three hours before Slick shot at him. If he had been alive, the one bullet alone that penetrated his heart would have soaked his nightclothes with blood. When the body was examined there was little or no trace of bleeding from any of the wounds.'

Captain Luke Dollar's gray eyes concentrated on Carl Mabee's arrogant and nearly bloodless face. 'You were unusually smart. Mr. Mabee,' he said evenly. 'But not quite smart enough. You killed Clifton McGowan. You saw to it that the oxygen tank which he used quite often when his heart bothered him, was filled with carbon monoxide instead of life-giving oxygen.'

'I sincerely hope you can support that statement, Captain Dollar.' Mabee tried to shrug the accusation off as valueless. 'I've never heard anything so ridiculous. Carbon monoxide gas indeed!'

'Let me give you and the rest of these people the story from the beginning,' Dollar suggested. 'It was your idea from the start to kill McGowan. You were deeply infatuated with Mrs. McGowan and she with you. As McGowan's attorney you knew that he was about to change his will, cutting off his wife as far as it was legally possible. His secretary informed you of the hiring of Slick to obtain evidence. You planted the gun in Slick's room at the Devonshire. We have two witnesses who saw you enter and leave Slick's room and we've traced the gun.'

Mabee was losing some of his self assurance. 'My gun indeed? I've never owned a revolver.'

'The gun was purchased in Chicago in 1908 by Sidney Sheller who one year later became your stepfather. After his death, the gun became the property of your mother. It has been in her possession until the day you removed it from her desk, purchased fresh ammunition at a sporting goods store on Vine Street, and hid it in Slick's clothing.

'As for the carbon monoxide gas, Mr. Mabee, there is enough comes out of the exhaust of a car in a couple of hours to kill several people. You emptied the tank of oxygen and with the aid of a high pressure pump, filled it with gas from your exhaust. Traces of the gas were found in the pump and the hose and your prints were on the tank.

'Daniel Slick was nothing more than a patsy. Mrs. McGowan bewitched him to the extent that he agreed to kill her husband in the fond expectation that she would marry him and he would thereby gain access to an estate of somewhere around two million dollars. McGowan was dead when

Slick entered that room, you knew it, and were waiting to slug him. You intended to kill him with that mallet. You came close, Mr. Mabee. Very close.'

Dollar shifted his gaze to Mrs. McGowan's downcast face. 'Would you care to enlarge on that, Mrs. McGowan?' he asked softly. 'We in this room can't of course promise anything. The jury and the judge will have to decide that. All I can say is what we tell other suspects. Co-operation with the authorities is taken into consideration by the judge.'

Mabee's face showed that he knew he was caught. His eyes shifted from the D.A.'s face to Captain Dollar's, then back to concentrate on Dan. In his eyes was all the hate that only a thwarted and frustrated man could feel.

Cleo McGowan lifted her head and her eyes seemed to suddenly light up with hatred. She wasted no time in accepting Captain Dollar's suggestion. She named Mabee as the master mind behind the plot and she insisted that everything that had been done had been because of his threats to ruin her life unless she did as he ordered. She even swore that she had loved her husband, that she despised Carl Mabee.

It was like a soaking cold rag slapped across Mabee's face. 'You stinking, two-timing devil!' he hurled at her.

Dan was directly across the room from both of them and he was the first one to see the switch knife that seemed to leap into Mabee's hand. He tried to fling himself across the intervening table and to grab Mabee's wrist. The table was too wide and he didn't have the time. The knife was in Cleo McGowan's back before he could reach Mabee's wrist. After that he was trying to avoid the wicked blade himself.

A gun exploded in the room, the sound of it beating against Dan's ears. Mabee's arm relaxed and the knife clattered to the floor. Dan's right hand was wet with blood and he looked at it stupidly, until someone placed a tourniquet around his wrist and helped him back into his chair.

All around him was confusion, men running in and out of the door. A physician hurried in with a small bag. He gave Mrs. McGowan a cursory examination, then shook his head. He looked at Mabee's face and said something about someone being an excellent shot. Then he moved to Dan. The blade had sliced open his palm to the bone. The doctor gave Dan a shot of whiskey, then took six stitches that Dan scarcely felt.

'If the blade was reasonably clean,' he said, 'the hand will be okay in a few weeks.'

Order was gradually growing out of turmoil. Dan sat in his chair, feeling his hand begin to throb, and wishing that someone would give him another drink, and wondering what was next on the program. As far as he knew he was still classified as a killer.

The District Attorney settled that in a short and stifflipped speech. 'There is no law in this state that penalizes a man for mutilating a corpse. There are some counties with statutes that cover it, but none in this one. Even if there was such a statute the penalty would not be as excessive as I should wish it might be.'

He glared at Dan. 'Your intentions, Daniel Slick, were to kill. But for the fact your victim was already dead, you would have been tried for murder, undoubtedly convicted and sentenced to die in the gas chamber. In the eyes of the law you are innocent. In the eyes of God you are as guilty as hell. Get out. You're a free man, much to my deepest regret.'

Captain Dollar rode the elevator with him to the ground floor. Before they parted Dan said, 'Thanks, Captain. I don't know what else to say.'

Dollar grinned at him. 'From now on keep your nose clean, Slick. And hunt up that Eddie Goes. There's a real woman. I wouldn't be surprised a bit she'd marry you if you asked her again. Women do beat all sometimes. They'll stick to a man they love no matter how big a jerk he is. So long, Slick.'

Dan turned his face south. He didn't have a dime in his pocket, but he had some in that safety deposit box and if he could just convince Eddie, there was still hope.

THE END